SHOTS FIRED

Detectives must find a murder weapon to close a cold case

IAN ROBINSON

Published by The Book Folks

London, 2021

© Ian Robinson

ISBN 978-1-913516-77-2

www.thebookfolks.com

Shots Fired is the third book in the DI Pippa Nash and DS Nick Moretti mystery series. Details about the other books can be found at the back of this one.

PROLOGUE

Blue and white tape fluttered like bunting in the brisk Scottish breeze. The cordon spanned the entire recreation area and playground that was situated between two residential tower blocks. Uniformed officer, PC McLachlan, stood outside the makeshift barrier. She was getting a sore throat. A result of continually having to explain to the residents that they should remain behind the tape. Nothing to see here – a lie and they all knew it. They knew it because the area would never see decoration unless a crime had been committed or it was a new mural of graffiti on a fresh section of wall.

Then there was the gunfire they'd heard.

The sound had echoed off the concrete and across the estate. The unmistakable repetition of a discharged firearm. The roundabout their children enjoyed was now occupied by the lifeless body of a young adult male. He was draped across the safety bar of the apparatus and his feet were angled in such a way that it appeared he'd lost the will to push.

Blood had leaked across the chipped metal paintwork and dripped to the floor where it had pooled. Two brass bullet casings twinkled in the low evening sun in contrast to the dark rubber safety matting the play equipment was affixed to. The crowd began to fluctuate in numbers. Some drifted away to be replaced by others as word got out. All transfixed at the sight of death. The PC crossed her arms and prayed the suits would soon arrive, bringing a tent and the forensic team to start collating evidence. A serial of uniform officers had joined her to assist with crowd control. PC McLachlan had done all she could and made the scene sterile. The clear skies had begun to darken, and she feared that if the tent wasn't here soon, rain might wash away anything of evidential value.

Chapter One

Detective Inspector Pippa Nash stared down at the parade square from her office window. She was gutted that she'd had to park on the other side of the office blocks that surrounded the Hendon training school site because it was beginning to rain.

She caressed the leaf of a trailing geranium between her thumb and index finger. She had inherited the plant three years earlier from a man she respected – a detective inspector who had been the previous occupant of her office and was now retired. The plant he too had inherited from his predecessor on the Homicide and Serious Crime Command where Nash worked. It was gifted to her when it was announced she was taking up his post. His thirty years now complete, his parting words to Nash were, 'If you can keep this plant alive in this place, then you're winning.'

The ring of her office phone broke her concentration. She left her horticultural pursuit and answered it.

'Nash, Homicide – team two,' she said. The voice on the end of the line wasn't one she recognised; such was the broad Glaswegian accent that replied.

'I've got the right detective, that's always a good start. DI Gordon, Glasgow Central. I have a job for you,' he said.

Nash sat down. 'Well, that's very kind of you to offer, DI Gordon, but I'm quite happy where I am,' she said.

Gordon gave a guttural laugh.

'Very good. Have you not seen the news?' he replied.

Nash sighed. 'No. I can't say I have. I've been rather busy with the fallout of overnight violence in London. How can I help you?' she asked.

She could hear DI Gordon was shuffling papers.

'Well, you're about to get busier. I've picked up a new murder and your name has been mentioned,' he said, in the abrupt way he'd address a suspect.

Nash leant on her desk, cradling the phone between her neck and jaw. She accessed the BBC news feed on her computer as she spoke.

'Look, is this some kind of joke? I'm really not in the mood so if you're one of Moretti's mates from up north then get on with your work,' she said.

DI Gordon had been up all night and his tone showed it.

'Look, missy. I haven't the time to be messing about. I'm calling you because an incident that's taken place on my patch is linked to one of yours in London,' he said.

Nash sat back. 'Go on.'

'Three years ago, you investigated a murder. A male called Scott Whittaker was shot and killed but no gun was recovered or suspect arrested,' he said.

'I'm listening,' replied Nash. She knew the case he was referring to. It had been a bugbear of hers that she hadn't nicked or charged anyone. Whittaker was, by all accounts, an innocent member of the public. A case of mistaken identity.

'The gun that was used to kill your victim has surfaced on my manor, Detective Inspector, and I don't like that. So when will you be in a position to liaise with me on your investigation?' he said, with an air of authority that Nash didn't like.

'DI Gordon, while I have every sympathy that you've picked up a new job, allegedly, with links to one of mine—'

'You can cut the attitude. There's no "allegedly" about it. The bullet recovered from my victim was fired from the same gun as the one involved in your murder. I'm not saying you will take my investigation on, but there might be something here in the ballistic report that you can use, hence my call. I believe in direct handover and not via a telephone line or email,' he said.

Nash rattled a pen between her teeth as she thought. She could insist he send it by recorded delivery or courier if he was so concerned it would get lost. Nash needed to see the report, but she also wanted to see the scene, assess if there were any similarities to the one she'd investigated. That was something that couldn't be established properly from a case file. The scene in Glasgow was recent, and an early look-over to find anything that correlated with her enquiry into the murder of Scott Whittaker would be beneficial. Problem was, due to the volume of work they had going on as a team, she'd been told to avoid taking on new cases if she could help it. The Whittaker case wasn't new either. It had been put in deep freeze but was perhaps beginning to thaw.

'I'll see you at your office tomorrow morning,' she said, after she took down the address DI Gordon provided.

She set her pen down just as the unmistakable scent of cheap Italian cologne wafted past her open door. A scent that she associated with one member of her staff, DS Nick Moretti.

'Nick, in here!' she shouted.

Moretti walked backwards and entered the frame of her door.

'I'm on it, I'm on it. Just grabbing a coffee before I have to face all the statements,' he replied. An empty mug dangled from his curled index finger.

'The paperwork can wait. Fire up the Ford. We're off to Glasgow on an overnighter,' she said.

Moretti's brow creased.

'How long have you been wanting to use that phrase?' he said, smiling as he spoke.

Nash pursed her lips and raised her eyebrows as she swayed in her swivel chair.

'What's so urgent we have to drop everything to go up north?' he asked.

Nash offered a chair opposite her. Moretti strode over to her Nespresso machine and filled his empty mug. He sat and listened as Nash explained the call.

'Do we have to drive?' he asked, with the look of a child faced with a day of maths at school.

'We'll fly and hire a car when we arrive. I'll leave it with you to make all the bookings for the plane. I'll sort the hotel and car,' she said.

'Don't trust me with it all?' Moretti replied.

'It's not that, Nick, but the last time I left it with you to make the arrangements we ended up in a flea pit for a hotel in a known area for prostitution. The car you hired was about as practical as a chocolate fireguard,' she said.

She scanned the news screen on her computer until she found a report of the shooting in Glasgow.

Moretti ignored her barbed comments and stared over her shoulder. There was an image of a PC on the crime scene and the obligatory shot of the blurred tent in the background that covered the body. Other than that, there was very little information. Moretti leant back.

'What do you hope to gain from this trip other than a hangover?' he asked, taking a sip of his coffee.

Nash dimmed the screen.

'I'm hoping we might establish another link to the Whittaker murder beyond what DI Gordon already has. He's saying the bullet recovered from his victim was fired from the same gun used on Whittaker. That gun being an Italian Beretta pistol. One that's been shared among the criminal fraternity like a packet of cigarettes. I thought the gun had been destroyed, as it hasn't been fired in three years, as far as we know. I had a contact flag created at the National Ballistic Intelligence Service. They have a hub in

Strathclyde and DI Gordon must have liaised with them on his job hence the call to me.'

Her mind was apace with what she could recall of Whittaker's murder. Moretti hadn't been involved in that investigation. It was one Nash had picked up while on Operation Trident, a unit that investigated gang-related shootings. Nash had agreed to keep the case when she'd transferred to the Homicide Command.

She looked at Nick, who was busy making notes in an A4 size daybook.

'I'll get on it then, Pip, and let you know once all the flights are booked,' he said.

Nash agreed she'd do the same with the hotel and hire car. She'd just finished making the arrangements when Moretti returned.

Nash looked up from her desk.

'All done. We fly at 5 p.m. so if it's all right with you I need to pop home and make sure I have everything packed,' he said.

Nash nodded in agreement. He could work from there until the flight. One of the advantages of a secure remote link to the HOLMES system.

Moretti tapped the woodwork that framed her door and left to organise himself before they flew.

Nash shouted after him. 'I'll drop by your place at two – we'll take a cab to the airport from there,' she said.

Moretti shouted back in acknowledgement. The marina where his boat was moored was close to City Airport. Nash could brief Moretti in the privacy of his boat before they flew. There weren't many perks to the job, but when you got the opportunity to travel, she'd always make the most of it.

Chapter Two

'You can drive,' Nash said, with a nod towards a red Nissan Micra in the Glasgow airport car park where they'd been advised to collect their hire car.

Moretti rubbed his stubbled chin and sighed.

'I don't think I'll fit in it,' he said, motioning his hands up and down his six-foot-seven frame.

Nash could contain herself no longer. She held her hand over her mouth to stifle a laugh.

'It's not this car is it?' Moretti questioned.

Nash shook her head. Her ponytail swayed as the tears streamed down her cheeks at the sight of her DS. A man who was usually self-assured looked mortified at the prospect of visiting another force in the red Micra. He let out a sigh of relief, with a hope the alternative would be better. They both turned at the sound of an engine. A midnight black BMW estate pulled up alongside them. The hire firm's representative established Nash as the recipient, and they all inspected the car for damage. Satisfied all was in order, she signed the hire agreement and accepted the keys, throwing them to Moretti with a smile.

'Shall we go?' she said.

Moretti slid into the driver's seat and wriggled his butt to get comfortable while he stroked the dashboard. His jawline taut in a smile.

'Good skills, Pip,' he said as they both belted up and set off towards the exit from the car park. 'So where to?' he asked, turning onto the trunk road towards the city.

Nash was keen to attend the scene of the shooting before she met with DI Gordon rather than going straight to his office as he'd asked. She always preferred to have eyes on any scene than have the information third hand.

'Let's go to the scene – here's the postcode for the estate,' she said, handing Moretti a piece of in-flight serviette with the postcode scrawled upon it.

He punched the number into the satnav and passed the serviette back to Nash. She stuffed the napkin into her coat pocket, feeling like a mother on a road trip. She'd considered giving DI Gordon a courtesy call before they both waltzed in but stopped herself. If the crime scene tape was still in place, then police would also be present. That was where she'd make her introductions and hear any word on the street prior to DI Gordon's arrival.

The city of Glasgow had the urban feel of London, but without the volume of people. The stop and start of the traffic, the multitude of shops, and the altercations between motorists brought her comfort.

They passed restaurants and shops, but her mind wasn't on eating or shopping; it was on the Beretta. Where had it been in the three years since the murder of Whittaker, and why had it suddenly arrived on the streets of Glasgow?

The weapon had been the subject of intensive research by scientists and NABIS. The theory was that it was such a prized instrument, it attracted a high price for hire within the criminal fraternity. She knew a firearm like this would be treated as precious goods. It wouldn't be handed out to anyone with an itchy trigger finger. The controller of the gun would want it back under their protection. Guns were getting harder to come by and a reliable weapon with a steady supply of ammunition was a hallowed article even if considered dirty through use in crime.

* * *

The satnav announced they were five minutes away from the estate. The cityscape changed from one of prosperity to one of poverty. No one living here would be thinking about eating out. Most would be concerned with when or how they'd acquire food for their families when they had no money to speak of.

'Choose somewhere reasonable to dump the car. We'll walk the rest of the way,' she said.

Moretti nodded and sought a place to park. Nash wanted to get a feel for the place on foot before she saw DI Gordon or the final murder scene. She wanted to understand the community and the issues they faced.

Moretti parked down a side street where he felt the vehicle would be safe, especially with all their luggage still being in it. He activated the alarm and pulled the collar of his coat around his neck as a bracing wind hit his face. He needed a smoke, but now wasn't the time to light his pipe as the wind was too strong.

Nash had taken the opportunity of borrowing a Paul Smith scarf from Moretti's boat. It was wrapped firmly around her neck and drawn up over her chin and nose. She made use of the deep pockets of her coat and stuffed her hands in as she strode ahead. Moretti caught up with her, thanks to his long stride. They arrived at the entrance to a parade of shops and behind them loomed a quad of tower blocks. They walked through the parade and became conscious of eyes on them.

The voyeurs ducked out of sight while a few remained propping up the walls; their cheeks withdrawing into their skulls as they inhaled smoke. Moretti breathed in the unmistakable sweet, earthy aroma of cannabis. A youth with a reefer remained stoic in his disposition and kept his blood-shot eyes locked on them.

Nash and Moretti blanked him. At the end of the walkway there was a noticeboard. Upon it was a map of the estate with an arrow showing where they were and the various names of the blocks. Nash found the name of the block they required, and they both continued.

As they entered the estate, Nash heard the unmistakable sound of a crime scene. She'd put money on any detective in the world knowing the sound of cordon tape flapping in a breeze. It was as though they'd entered a kite festival, but without the aerial view. The tent was gone. A lone uniform officer was gathering up spent plastic barrier tape and dumping the remnants in a rubbish bin.

'You can cross it now – we're done,' the officer said.

Nash and Moretti approached the last vestiges of what had been the cordon. A single section of tape stretched between two rubbish bins. A gaggle of children sat upon the same roundabout the body must have been on. The clean-up, over. Nash was surprised it still worked as there was rust all over it, along with flaking paintwork.

'They quickly adapt, don't they?' the officer said, nodding in the direction of the youngsters who clambered over the equipment like a swarm of ants on a fresh carcass. 'Youse are from London? DI Gordon never said you'd be coming over to the crime scene.'

The officer pushed the final scraps of tape into the bin before topping it off with her latex gloves.

Nash sensed that word of their arrival would have already filtered back to Gordon. DI Gordon would have eyes and ears on the estate with a direct line to his office, she thought.

'I'm DI Nash and this is DS Moretti.'

'I'm PC McLachlan. I'm the beat officer for the estate tasked with clearing up the shit no one else will touch,' she said, raising her eyes as she spoke. Nash took advantage of the contact.

'So, what's the word on the street?' she asked.

'Not here,' the officer said, indicating with a motion of her head that they should follow her.

PC McLachlan led them back to the parade of shops they'd just left and stopped outside a unit that was central to the parade. Nash and Moretti had missed it earlier having been distracted by the reefer-smoking onlooker. The Police Scotland emblem stretched across the window.

A combination of Thistle, Royal crown, and the Latin phrase, *Semper Vigilo* – always alert. PC McLachlan produced her key and opened the main door to the police office.

'Drink?' she asked, dumping her hat and utility belt on a chair. Nash and Moretti acknowledged they'd love one.

They all sat within a room that had the feel of an interview and statement taking area. It was comfortable enough. A few armchairs, a table, and hard seats for more formal situations. Nash thanked the PC for the tea and sat in a comfy chair. After all the travelling, she welcomed the warmth of the tea and a plate of shortbread biscuits.

Nash wanted the officer settled before the questions began. She would get the answers she wanted though and if that meant ruffling feathers then so be it. Time would tell how responsive Police Scotland would be to her requests for information.

'So, a busy time for you then?' Nash said.

McLachlan nodded. 'You could say that. I think this shooting has upset folk. Look, they put up with the drug dealing, but they don't like it when people get gunned down.'

'What's your take on it… I'm sorry I don't know your first name?' Nash said.

'Kelly,' she replied.

'Pippa, but you can call me Pip, and this is Nick.'

McLachlan smiled at them both.

'I've never called a DI by their first name. Not DI Gordon, anyway,' she said.

Nash smiled warmly and McLachlan continued just as Nash desired.

'I'm trusted on the estate – for an officer. I treat the people like I'd expect to be treated and they respect that. They also know I won't take any shite,' she said, leaning for the box of shortbread.

Nash pushed it across to her with a smile.

'Yesterday a local approached me when I was on patrol. It wasn't long after the shooting. I knew that he wanted to talk. You can sense it and when you know someone around here, you just know. We agreed on a place to talk and met there. He looked shaky and more so than normal. He told me he wants to talk about the shooting, but he insists he never witnessed what happened.' McLachlan paused.

Like hell he didn't see anything, Nash thought. McLachlan continued.

'He reckons he saw a motorbike cruising around the streets on the outskirts of the estate. He thought it was surveillance police, but then he noticed the yellow bib the rider was wearing and dismissed it. The bike disappeared and then he saw it again. The rider had picked someone up. He thought it must be a motorcycle instructor teaching. The bike went away and then he heard shots. By the time he got to the scene, the bike had gone. He could see the body on the roundabout and made off.'

McLachlan finished and looked at the two detectives both of whom remained impassive as they listened to her account.

Nash was the first to speak.

'Can you get hold of this guy again? I'd like to speak with him.'

McLachlan looked to the floor then back at Nash. 'Not without DI Gordon being there. I don't know how you do things, but DI Gordon knows this contact and has insisted I don't speak with him again until he's with me. It's all been recorded properly with our source unit.'

Nash nodded in appreciation of the circumstances and logged it in her mind to pursue the possible lead. She'd go through her own source unit. A handler known to all as the Silverfox would have greater clout in getting the information she needed. Despite her rank, his world was one of secrecy, and protocol was there to protect and not exploit. His sources' information had proven beneficial in the past and Nash had to establish any issues that may affect the line of enquiry regarding the Beretta.

'Is there another tea, Kelly?' Nash asked.

Kelly got up and gathered all the mugs keen on a change of scenery. Nash followed her into a kitchen area.

'Have you worked here long?' Nash asked, while McLachlan found a fresh lot of tea bags.

'Five years. Long enough to know when someone is telling me the truth or not, Pip,' she said.

'I didn't mean it like that. You know these streets better than me. Any names offered up or anywhere you think the gun could be laid down?'

'Nothing. Everyone's in shock. Not about the murder, that isn't a rarity, but the way it's been done is. Guns play a part here, but not like this. Not in a kiddie park. There are laws on the street and slaying people where kids are about is off limits in these parts,' she said. The kettle boiled and McLachlan went about making the tea. 'Do you like nightclubs?' she asked, casually.

'No, but my DS does,' Nash replied.

'There's an emergency services night on in Glasgow at ten. Shame to waste an evening stuck in a hotel,' McLachlan said.

Nash took a business card from McLachlan.

'If your DS fancies it then here's my number. He can share his with me and I'll text the details,' she said.

Nash returned to where Moretti was sitting and waited for McLachlan to bring the drinks through.

'Here's McLachlan's mobile number. She's going clubbing tonight – your lucky day,' she said, her head tilting as she widened her eyes.

Moretti looked like the cat who'd got the cream as he accepted the card and turned it over in his fingers.

They waited for McLachlan to return to her seat. Nash was keen to ask a few more questions before DI Gordon realised that they'd arrived and were on scene. The main door to the office beeped. McLachlan got up and walked towards the reception where a stentorian voice shattered the party.

'PC McLachlan, a wee birdie told me you had the kettle on and a couple of guests, I believe,' said the voice in a tone and abrupt manner that Nash immediately recognised as being that of DI Gordon.

Gordon swept past McLachlan, taking the biscuit she was carrying as he strode past. He entered the room where Nash and Moretti sat. In his other hand he carried a buff folder which he dropped onto the coffee table.

'Well now, what have we here? Two detectives from The Smoke, I believe?' Gordon said, flopping down into McLachlan's seat. He picked up her mug of tea and took a sip, then looked back at his PC. 'Splosh more milk and three sugars, please,' he said, handing her the mug.

Nash smacked her lips at his floorshow.

'I'm sorry, did I miss something?' Gordon asked.

Nash stared at him with a look of dismay.

'Only your mouth,' she replied, nodding at the array of shortbread crumbs that were scattered across Gordon's tie and had come to rest in the creases of his Italian-fit shirt.

Gordon wasn't one for exercise, unlike Moretti. Gordon ran his tongue over his tobacco-stained teeth.

'I don't respond well to detectives from out-of-town taking it upon themselves to nosy around my patch,' Gordon said, accepting the mug of tea from McLachlan who made herself scarce.

Moretti coughed and stood up. 'I need a pee,' he said, and walked towards the toilet door.

Nash leant forward in contrast to Gordon's slouched state; her tongue resting between her teeth as she readied herself for confrontation.

'Yesterday, when you contacted me, you were insistent that your incident was linked to a case of mine. Well here I am. If, along the way, I'm fortunate enough to meet the beat officer who patrols the estate then I would do what

I'd expect any decent detective to do – talk to them,' she said. She sat back and cradled her Police Scotland mug.

Gordon gave a huff in reply and pushed over the docket he'd dropped onto the table.

'A copy of the ballistic report, as promised. It contains details of the bullet extracted from the victim and a link with casing found at the scene,' Gordon said. He sat back and watched while Nash picked up the docket and opened it.

'Is this it?' Nash asked with incredulity at the single sheet of paper the docket contained.

'What more do you want?' Gordon replied.

Nash closed the docket and placed it between the chair cushion and frame. In truth, she hadn't expected much more, but she knew by this visit that she wouldn't be seeing any incident room if one existed at all. She imagined DI Gordon was a one-man band with a team of merry men to do as instructed. She was no Maid Marian though.

'Well, if you've nothing further to add then my visit is concluded, DI Gordon,' Nash said, and stood up taking her coat from the back of the chair just as Moretti returned.

Gordon stood up.

'Be seeing you, sir,' Moretti said, before he joined Nash and they both left Gordon in the office. PC McLachlan had already returned to her patrol.

Nash and Moretti turned left out of the police office and walked back to the car. Moretti glanced up at the grey sky.

'Was it something we said?' Moretti asked, adjusting his collar against the rain, as they crossed the road from the shops.

'It was what we didn't say, Nick.'

Moretti looked perplexed.

'Please or thank you,' Nash followed up.

Chapter Three

Nash glanced over the front page of *The Herald* and sipped her coffee. As she read the front page, she learnt more about the shooting than during the brief moments she'd had with DI Gordon. Moretti appeared at the door to the restaurant area where breakfast was served, and a waitress walked him over to Nash's table. He sat down and ordered a fresh pot of coffee. Nash looked up and then returned to her paper as she spoke.

'You look like death,' she said.

Moretti poured himself a coffee from the nearly spent carafe Nash had been using. He pushed his fingers through his thatch of dark hair and Nash looked over her paper and noted he was still dressed in the same clothes he'd worn the night before when he'd left her at the bar to meet PC McLachlan at the nightclub. Nash had opted to enjoy the facilities of the hotel rather than a Glasgow club with officers she didn't know.

'Please... Pip, the only grilling I need is one from the breakfast buffet,' he said.

The waitress returned with Moretti's coffee pot and took his breakfast order after setting Nash's full Scottish breakfast before her.

'I hope she was worth it. What did you learn?' Nash asked, putting the paper down and cutting into a tattie scone.

Moretti's skin turned a whiter shade of pale and Nash wondered whether he was about to throw up, but he soon recovered enough to talk. She knew he'd sober up quickly. He always did once he'd eaten and taken on-board a jug coffee.

'In regard to your first statement, I never kiss and tell,' he said, with a childish grin.

Nash shook her head and the dimples in her cheeks became pronounced.

'I did learn that our friend Mr Gordon isn't as hostile as he came across. Word is he's under pressure to see this job put to bed quick and he's like you – thorough,' Moretti said. His breakfast now arrived. He slathered it in brown sauce and continued his conversation while he ate.

'He said he'd call me if, and when, they get a suspect. I believe Gordon was being honest. He took my card.'

Nash huffed at this comment, as if a business card ever guaranteed a call back. Whatever happened to decent old-school civility? In the Met a visiting detective would be met at the airport, official business conducted, before they were wined and dined at the best curry house London had to offer and sent home with a Met police crest and a hangover.

Moretti was beginning to get the colour back in his face as he ate.

'One thing though,' he said, emphasising the statement with his fork. 'The motorbike McLachlan mentioned being involved they've got no index plate for. They do have CCTV of the bike in the area. It showed a second male being scooped up. The rider McLachlan's fella said he saw, wasn't the rider but the pillion,' Moretti said, as he set down his knife and fork and wiped his mouth on the cotton serviette.

'Do you ever stop to breathe while you eat?' Nash asked.

Moretti wasn't looking at her, his eyes were trying to track the attention of the waitress.

'I'm starving, ma'am – Pip,' he stammered.

A waitress arrived, and he ordered two orange juices and a round of toast. Nash let out a sigh as she watched Moretti concentrating on the waitress as she walked away.

Nash clicked her fingers near his ear, and his head snapped back to her.

'When can we see the CCTV?' she asked.

'I'll have it sent to Owen back at the office,' Moretti said.

Owen being DS Owen Matthews who managed the Intelligence Desk on Nash's Homicide team. He and DC Jones had been re-instated following an unwarranted enquiry by professional standards who found both detectives to have acted lawfully when Matthews had smashed a work car into a robbery team's moped, pinning two suspects under it during an armed robbery.

'Did you read the file Gordon left you?' Moretti asked.

'I did. The rifling on the bullet has been linked to the Beretta used in our murder. What it isn't telling me is where that gun has been laid down for the three years it hasn't been seen on the street,' Nash said.

Moretti leant back in his chair. He too hadn't a clue where such a gun would be kept, and it was looking like a tall order to find out.

Nash gave him a look that Moretti knew meant it was time to leave the comforts they were enjoying.

'Get your stuff and let's get back to London,' she said.

Moretti looked out of the large windows onto the busy Glasgow streets and wished he could stay a while longer. He rubbed his face in his hands, downed the orange juice in one slug, and they both left the restaurant to get packed and catch their flight back to London.

Chapter Four

Nash felt relieved to be back within the familiar territory of her office. She'd arrived early, coffee in hand, to prepare for her team's arrival for an eight o'clock briefing. She heard the voices of her detectives resonating along the corridor as she ensured the briefing room was ready.

Nash had looked forward to this day. The day she would resurrect Operation Aurora, the murder of Scott Whittaker. She'd been keen to seek closure for the family ever since the case had dried. Scott was a driver for a nationwide vehicle recovery service. Never sick and well respected within his organisation. Letters of appreciation from stranded motorists were a common occurrence at the recovery firm's office. Nash was confident she'd provide closure for the family now the murder weapon had resurfaced.

She took her mug and walked out to the briefing room. She was met with a chorus of *good mornings* and some wry comments about how Moretti had coped while they were away. She looked around the table and was pleased to see her inside team were present: George Sagona the office manager, DS Owen Matthews her Intelligence DS and Sally Clarke, an analyst whose work had proved pivotal in a recent investigation. JJ strode in and took his usual seat along with a dishevelled-looking DC Jones and Moretti. Other detectives filed in and soon the room was full. Nash brought the meeting to order and clicked an infrared pointer at the projector screen that flashed up a CCTV frame. She waited for the voices to die down and the eyes of the room to concentrate on her.

'Good morning. You all know any initial briefing can involve a lot of information and I hope to be as succinct as I can,' Nash said, while she pressed her keyboard and let the CCTV play.

She let the footage run while she spoke, all her team's focus now shifted from her to the CCTV.

'We're looking at the footage provided by Police Scotland in relation to the fatal shooting of a young male know as Calvin Smalls. Smalls is known to Glasgow police. He's a drugs runner for an organised criminal network that control significant-sized cannabis grow houses. I've been notified by DCI Carlson that there's rumour of a live operation looking at the problem. He doesn't know which agency, but it isn't us or Police Scotland,' she said. 'Owen, I need you to do some digging to establish who's got oversight and control of that operation, police that is, not criminal. I appreciate it's probably been designated as a Confidential Operation. Do your best.'

Owen nodded and Nash continued.

'The image you're looking at has been taken from a covert camera. The camera was being used to combat fly tipping. It shows a motorbike and rider in this section of footage. In the next frame, taken some five minutes later, we can see the same bike but with a passenger. This bike hasn't been seen in the area until now. The council installed the camera, and it's been running for over two weeks. The bike does not appear on the system until the day of the murder.

'Calvin Smalls was shot twice. Once to the torso and then to the head at close range. Two minutes after the incident the bike is gone. It was picked up again here.' Nash drifted the laser pointer over a section of motorway. 'The bike then leaves the area and is lost. Enquiries are underway by Police Scotland to try to trace the bike after it left the estate.'

Nash paused while her team caught up with notes they felt were useful.

Sagona was the first to pipe up with a question. Nash had expected it. He was the gatekeeper for the HOLMES system running the main actions for their investigation to ensure the right detective got the work and the same line of enquiry wasn't duplicated.

'So how is this relevant to us? It isn't clear that these two on the bike had anything to do with it,' Sagona asked. His fingers interlaced against his straining waist.

'I was coming to that but as you've asked – you're right. It's a motorbike in the area prior to the shooting. It's been designated as a vehicle to be traced and eliminated from the investigation. However, the shell casings recovered at the scene are a different issue. They are very relevant to us. The forensic examination of the casings was fast-tracked by DI Gordon from Glasgow and the results are in this docket.'

Nash tapped the docket on the table in front of her before she continued.

'The rifling on the bullets recovered from Smalls' body match with the type of bullet and rifling recovered at Scott Whittaker's scene in Operation Aurora. I've read the ballistics report. They were fired from the same gun.'

Nash pressed the clicker again and an image of a pistol appeared.

'It's believed that the weapon we are seeking is this: a 9 mm Beretta 9000s. Not just any old gun. It has a history. It's been forensically linked to nine firearms incidents across London. It's never been recovered. It was last recorded being used in the murder of Scott Whittaker. Since then, it appears to have been unused – until now, obviously,' Nash said. All eyes were on the image of the firearm.

'I've no intention of going into the features of the gun. Fact is, in the right hands, it works and is back on the street. I need that weapon found, and a suspect attached to it. Before you all start blathering on about it being in Scotland and nothing to do with us – save it. It has everything to do with us,' Nash said. On the screen was an image of Scott Whittaker slumped by the floor of his truck; blood pooled at his feet as a result of a large hole in his skull.

'This is Scott Whittaker. Scott was a vehicle recovery driver and on 28 August 2018 he was in London doing his job only to be gunned down. I did all I could with my old team to bring the shooter to justice. All we had in the end amounted to three spent shells at the scene and bullets that were 9 mm and fired from a Beretta 9000s. Help me to find Scott's killer and get this case closed. To business. Owen, establish a link with Scotland. I want updates on their investigation. George, access the case history on the HOLMES computer for Operation Aurora and go back through it with Moretti. Look for any gaps or investigative opportunities missed. In the meantime, I want any outstanding actions from all our current cases turned around as quickly as possible please. I have a bad feeling that the Beretta's resurrection is going to bring the pains on in more ways than one. That's all,' she said.

Her team extracted themselves from their seats and began to drift back to their own zones.

Nash scooped up the ballistic report, and looked up at the screen. The enlarged image of the barrel of the Beretta stared back at her. She blinked and felt her heart rate increase as she happily turned off the projector. She made her way along the corridor and back to her office where she walked to the window, picked up a spent plastic water bottle and tipped the remainder into the trailing geranium. She knew who she'd have to visit next, and it was a visit she didn't relish.

Chapter Five

Moretti hummed *Going Underground* by The Jam as he and Nash descended the stairs to the tube station. Nash had contacted Scott Whittaker's wife, Lorraine Whittaker, who'd said she wouldn't be home until after four that afternoon as she had the nursery run to do. The child had been just a baby when Nash first picked up the investigation three years ago. The tube platform was empty save for a couple loaded down with shopping bags after a trip to Brent Cross. The electronic sign blinked. The next train was in two minutes. Moretti turned to her.

'Tell me, with there being so many interested parties in the Beretta's life of crime, why is it only us paying any interest in the fact it's resurfaced?' Moretti asked.

Nash rubbed her temple.

'Because there's no prisoner attached to it – yet. That's why,' she said, staring across the tracks.

Moretti glanced at her.

'C'mon, it can't be that. Others, like us, must have been informed about the striation marks on the bullets. There were so many other cases,' Moretti said, his voice dipping in tone to a whisper.

Nash drew her lips to her teeth then released them.

'Nick, the shooting teams get these jobs all day long. It's the same shit different day. They arrive, assess, and investigate. If there's no one on the floor creating a new pond of claret, they're left with a scene of recovery. Recovery of shells, or bullets lodged in masonry or cars, forensics – you know the stuff. There are so many shootings in London that they cannot scramble to one in Scotland. I take your point though and I did make a call,' she said, as she watched the train approach.

The carriage drew up, and the doors slid open. They stepped in and found a dual seat.

Nash continued once the train moved off, leaning into Moretti as she spoke.

'There are other crimes linked to this weapon, as you surmised. Other victims as a result of the gun being fired. Some sustained injuries, life-changing injuries at that, but Scott Whittaker was the first to die. The victims that survived the other incidents are saying nothing. Trust me, we did a lot of work when it first came in, but nothing was forthcoming. No witnesses, no CCTV. Only the forensic matches from the bullets. All the casings found were clean. What's interesting about Glasgow's job is that there were two shots fired. Both hit the target, and by the close range to the head, it sounds like an execution. The shooter knew how to handle a gun. The other jobs were very much shut the eyes, squeeze the trigger, and hope,' she said, leaning away.

Moretti nodded his understanding. He had a mate on one of the shooting teams and understood what Nash was saying. This situation was different. The Beretta was with a different class of criminal.

They arrived at Lorraine Whittaker's address and Nash felt a sense of déjà vu as she pushed the intercom for Flat 6. There was no reply, and she tried it again. They both heard the click; the main door released, and they entered.

The Victorian house had been split into flats: basement, first, and second floor. The Whittakers lived on the top floor. They were met by a woman around five feet in height with French cropped hair and elfin features. She was carrying a little boy who began to wriggle and squirm once he'd seen who was at the door. Moretti gave him a big smile and the boy's eyes widened before he buried his head in his mum's shoulder. They were invited in and went into the living room. Lorraine Whittaker placed the toddler on the floor where he could amuse himself with a selection of toys.

The flat was as Nash remembered it on the night she'd attended with the Family Liaison Officer to break the news of Scott's death. Lorraine Whittaker had taken the news, as Nash had hoped, with a natural reaction and had continued to seem genuine as the enquiry progressed. Nash had been confident, at the time, that Lorraine had not been involved in the planning of the shooting, nor had she been the one to pull the trigger.

Framed photos of the three of them adorned the sideboard. Faces that told a story of happier times.

'Can I get you both a drink? Tea, coffee... water?' Lorraine asked.

'Tea would be great, Lorraine,' Nash said, and Moretti nodded in agreement.

Whittaker left the toddler with them and went to the kitchen where they heard the tap run and the sound of the kettle being turned on. Nash took in as much of the room as she could while she had the chance. She'd dealt with too many cases to remember everyone's home, but some stood out more than others. Each one had secrets on display even if the props were mute.

Nash was looking at a typical family home. It was relaxed and felt like a safe place to raise a child. A nurturing environment. There were signs of money: Smart TV from a big brand, music system the same – all wireless. From what Nash could see of the kitchen, Whittaker liked her KitchenAid appliances and there was the recognisable industrial shimmer of a quality toaster.

Lorraine came back carrying a set of Le Creuset mugs on an Orla Kiely designed tray. Lorraine wouldn't think to explore the value range as Nash might. Whittaker set the tray down and handed out the mugs of tea before she sat on the edge of a chair and watched little Fraser while he bashed the top of a spinning-top that lit up as it revolved.

'How have you been, Lorraine?' Nash asked, taking a sip of tea, observing Lorraine over the rim of the mug.

Whittaker relaxed into the seat and faced Nash.

'It's been tough, very tough. Every day I look at Fraser and I see Scott. Time isn't the great healer they claim,' she said with a weak smile.

Nash returned the gesture.

'I can't imagine. We're here because we need to talk again about the night Scott was killed and to update you. We've re-opened the enquiry,' Nash said.

Lorraine hunched forwards, the mug on her knees supported by her hands.

Nash noticed her eyes reacted pensively to the news – news that wouldn't have come as a surprise. Most people who are left behind after such a tragedy know that when the police call, they aren't popping in for a catch-up.

'There's been another incident, and we felt we should come and see you – to explain why we've re-opened Scott's case,' Nash said.

Whittaker screwed up her eyes.

'I never thought it was closed,' she replied, her demeanour of hostess now evaporated like the rising steam from her mug.

'A poor use of words, on my part, Lorraine. You're right. It had never gone away. We'd hit a period where we'd established all we could; but now we have a possible lead and we wish to pursue this,' Nash said.

Whittaker remained the same. Her body rigid as though she'd witnessed an unexplained phenomenon. Nash's mind recorded Lorraine's reaction. Victims' families never reacted the same way to the news of death or an update of an investigation. Their reactions were as unique as the murder. They all had a set of hopes as to what would be imparted. Most of the time those hopes were dashed.

'So what's the new lead?' Lorraine asked. Fraser's hands danced and dipped on his legs in front of her.

Nash was no expert where children were concerned, but if she sensed a change in the air, then she assumed the toddler must have too. Nash wasn't in the habit of revealing new evidence or leads as quickly as some of her colleagues, and she wasn't about to change now.

'At the moment we wish to keep the news confidential. It will help the investigation if it progresses. What I can tell you is that there *hasn't* been an arrest, I'm very sorry,' Nash said, and gave a weak smile as she finished.

Moretti remained a passive observer. A vital and underestimated role for any detective. The ability to listen rather than question.

'So you've come all this way for nothing?' Whittaker said, her eyes darting between the two detectives.

'I appreciate it may feel that way, but it wasn't something I wished to say over the phone,' Nash said.

Whittaker elevated Fraser into her arms and stood.

'In that case I can see no further purpose in you remaining here. Thanks for nothing,' she said, and walked through to the kitchen, leaving Nash and Moretti to see themselves out.

* * *

They left and returned to the tube station. The light was fading and Moretti scuffed alongside her as they walked.

'Out with it, Nick,' Nash said.

Moretti hitched his bag on his shoulder, stuffing his hands in the pockets of his long coat, which he was glad he'd brought as spots of rain began to decorate the grey fabric.

'Well she, Lorraine, is right in a way. Why did we visit her? We could have called or just sent an FLO,' he said.

Nash ducked under the cover of a bus shelter and Moretti joined her. The bus appeared in the distance and Nash recognised the number. It would take them back towards the incident room at Hendon.

'Let's get out of the wet,' she said, sticking her arm out as she spoke.

The bus pulled over. They got on and sat near the back. Nash leant into Moretti.

'Sometimes it's better to speak in person than on a phone. Gauge the other's reaction, even if it may appear you're not giving them much to react to,' she said. She spoke in a hushed voice close to his ear. Moretti reciprocated the permitted invasion of personal space.

'I get that – kind of, but it felt like we were winding her up back there – giving her false hope,' he said.

Nash sighed.

'There were unanswered questions at the time, Nick. Lifestyle questions, pertinent to Lorraine. She was very much a dark horse in an unlit stable. However, from what I saw today not a lot has changed,' Nash said, with a hint of resignation in her voice.

Moretti nodded. He could see the point in the visit now. Not fully, but he appreciated that sometimes a detective had to put in the shoe work to discover the missing pieces of the puzzle. Sometimes the effort paid off, other times not. It could be the time wasn't right for the big reveal. But this wasn't a reality TV weight loss programme. A life had been shed and the destruction and loss felt widely. With this case, neither Nash nor Moretti could tell where it would lead.

Nash looked out the window of the single deck bus. A street grimed vista streaked with rain. She recognised the outline of the rooftops of the Peel Centre base as the bus continued along Aerodrome Road. She pressed the bell, and the bus slowed to a halt at the next registered stop and they got off.

'One last thing,' Moretti said, pulling his coat around him as he ducked into the torrent of water that lashed his face.

'Yes?' Nash said, she too leant into the weather and pulled a scarf around her mouth and nose.

'Can we take the car in future?' he said, breaking into a slow trot towards the main gates to the site.

Nash tutted. 'No sense of adventure, Detective Sergeant,' she said.

They displayed their warrant cards to the gatekeeper in a quick sleight of hand before they ran across the parade square towards the doors of their building.

Chapter Six

DS Owen Matthews realised Nash had returned. He'd heard the distinctive sound of her quick-paced footfall along the tiled floor of the corridor to the incident room and wanted to ensure he was the first in line to update her.

Nash couldn't return to her office without a detective rapping on her door five minutes later demanding her attention. Today she really didn't need to be doorstepped. She was soaked and needed time to hang up the Barbour biker's coat she habitually wore. She loved it for its practicality and fit, and she could conceal her officer safety equipment in the pockets.

Matthews appeared at her door. He stepped back as Nash thrust a coffee pot towards him.

'Fill this up and then come back, Owen,' she said, handing him the pot.

He accepted it and shook his head as he headed towards the nearest tap to refill it. He felt like a probationer on his first night duty again. He returned and Nash accepted the water. She filled up the correct receptacle before she placed the pot under the drip feed.

'What do you have, Owen?' she asked, flicking on the system to boil.

'Oh, milk and two sugars would be lovely,' he said.

'I meant what police work do you have for me, Owen,' she replied. She sat behind her desk and shifted some paperwork that had been dumped upon it to one side.

Matthews shifted in his seat opposite; his face flushed. Nash kicked off her rain-soaked shoes and lamented the urban grime that caked the sides. She hoped the tepid air from the building's central heating system would dry out her skin tone tights. Nash could see Matthews had a folder, and she nodded at him to pass it over to her.

She opened it up. Within it were a series of crime scene photos from the murder in Glasgow. Matthews had received them by email and printed her out a copy – she liked to see them in print rather than on a screen. She flicked through the A4 size images. They always made grim viewing. Whoever fired the gun would have been stationary or a very good shot to hit the torso first. Very few people remained still long enough to see if the gun was real before making a decision to flee.

Any movement of the victim would have altered the bullet's trajectory. The shooter would have had a split second to get the shot off and must have been confident they'd be able to achieve it or fluked it. The second shot to the head was a given as Smalls would have been on the ground from the first. Highly unlikely to shoot to the head then the torso. It would have happened within seconds. Nash set the images aside, open on one of Smalls splayed out on the floor of the roundabout taken at a wider angle.

'Pretty gruesome viewing,' Matthews said, wiping his mouth on the back of his hand.

'Was there anything else, Owen?' Nash said, her tone level. Not as blunt as the question could be interpreted. Nash could tell by the look on his face and the way he remained seated that he had something he needed to get off his chest.

'Well, there's a lot of chatter out there,' he said, indicating with a nod of his head to the main incident room, 'that we're treading on toes... we have enough work on here without assisting Glasgow and their investigation.'

Nash had heard enough – first Moretti and now Matthews. There'd clearly been more talk than action going on in her incident room while she and Moretti were out.

'Round up the team. Briefing room, ten minutes, and I know they're all here, Owen, as the parade square's littered with our fleet vehicles,' she said. She stood up and straightened her skirt.

Matthews knew it was time to leave and did so without question, leaving the envelope and the images on the coffee table.

Nash waited for Matthews to vacate her room. She grabbed a spare pair of shoes and slipped them on. As she waited for her team to enter the briefing room, she reflected on whether they were right. They did have a lot of work outstanding, and this wasn't a new investigation to them but one she'd brought with her from another unit. She knew they'd all be thinking it would be best suited being passed back to the shooting team to investigate. Nash had brought the investigation with her for a reason – it was unfinished business which she had every intention of completing.

The murmur of voices subsided as she entered the room. All eyes were upon her. It was as though she'd walked in naked and in many ways, she felt like that.

She'd hoped her DSs would have quashed any perceived uprising at source before it arrived at her door to deal with. No such luck. She took up her position as head of the table and leant on the surface as she spoke.

'Right, it's been brought to my attention that some of you aren't happy with us providing distant assistance to the murder investigation in Glasgow. By distant, I mean so far away we could be classed as remote.'

She paused and dipped her head, taking a breath in an attempt to quash the anger that had arisen inside her.

The team was silent and attentive. Even George Sagona was quiet. Nash continued.

'I can only think that my initial briefing was too short. That maybe I'd underestimated the service levels in the room and the weight of detective ability among you. So, with that in mind, it's important that you're reminded about what our remit entails – murder. Now, some of you consider that we have enough in London without assisting our colleagues in the north, and I agree. However, the murder of a man in London doesn't disappear because it's three years old. That murder has now been injected with *new* and corroborative evidence. The only spanner in the works is that the evidence happens to have been found in Scotland. An incident involving the *same* gun that killed Scott Whittaker while he was assisting a member of the public.'

Nash was in full flow. She shifted from the head of the table and began to patrol the perimeter of the briefing room that was defined by the backs of her detectives, all of whom faced each other rather than look behind them. Their eyes flitting between themselves in furtive glances.

She recognised the look of impunity on Matthews's face when she'd asked him to get the water for the coffee machine. When she added that up with his feedback on how her unit felt about her decision making, she knew it was time to lay down the ethics of investigation according to Nash. She'd be damned if she'd let some crusty old DCs swing a wrecking ball at those ethics along with their lamps of old. She continued to walk, and her breathing settled as it did when she ran. The last thing she desired was to lose control in front of her team.

She needed them and they knew it. They also needed her, and she'd proved that on many an investigation.

Sagona could contain his urge to speak no longer.

'I understand that, ma'am,' he said, a certain smarm about the way he addressed her wasn't lost on Nash who admired Sagona's bravery to speak up. 'But we could wait until Scotland make an arrest and then we could… you know, assist.' Sagona mumbled the last word.

Nash stopped. 'I see. So what you're proposing, George, is let Police Scotland run with the job and only react when they say jump? Is that what I'm hearing? Is that what you all think?' Nash said, as she swayed her arms out wide as though she was acknowledging a round of applause.

Sagona shrugged.

'Because what happens with that style of detection, ladies and gentlemen, is that we get left with the crumbs,' Nash said. 'Crumbs that get ground into the shitty government issue carpet as a result of detectives thundering size tens tramping up to Scotland to claim first dibs at the prisoner. Scotland won't care – their job will be put to bed, done and dusted. Meanwhile, we're all scrambling to be first through the door and get the fella on the charge sheet before he decides to shut up and say nothing. Inundated with all the false promises of what the different forces can do for him in terms of reduction of sentence. I don't operate that way. I appreciate you don't know that as this is the first time this has happened since I took over as your DI. Now you know. If you have a problem investigating what *was* a cold case enquiry but is now *active,* then I'll assist you in any application you wish to make for an alternative post within the Met. Be mindful that the Homicide Command will *not* be an option. I refuse to support that attitude on any command I work within. Any other business?'

Nash took in the wide-eyed faces around the table. Heads were dipped, ready to leave, while others couldn't comprehend where the vitriolic response had come from. Nash cared little. She had a murder to investigate with every chance another murder could land on her desk.

When there were no other questions, she left the room, which was uncharacteristically quiet for the end of a meeting.

Nash heard a tap on her open door, and Moretti entered. He knew Nash well enough not to have to wait to be told he could. If she wasn't expecting any visitors, then her door would've been closed.

'I didn't have you down as the first to ask for a transfer,' Nash said.

She got up and closed the door, and Moretti sat down after he'd poured them both a coffee. Nash walked back to her desk and collapsed into her chair. The steam from the mug billowed out invitingly. Moretti said nothing and waited for Nash.

'I hate having to do that, Nick,' she said, pulling the mug towards her.

She kicked off her shoes again and Moretti sat back and crossed his legs.

'I know you do – but it needed saying. If I'd have been here, I'd have said the same thing and, Owen, with the best will in the world, isn't the type of DS to hit back at them,' Moretti said.

Nash dropped her head slowly, then raised it and stared at the ceiling. Her neck felt tense. Moretti got up and handed her a strip of paracetamol. She popped two and dry swallowed them, as the coffee was too hot.

'Thank you, Nick.'

She was going to tackle the paperwork on her desk when the phone rang. Moretti pointed at himself to answer it, which meant he'd make the excuses Nash wasn't available and get a contact for her to call back; but Nash picked it up.

'Nash, Homicide – team two,' she said.

A broad but softly spoken Northern Irish voice filtered through. As she listened, she pulled her daybook out of a pod drawer. She took a pen from a holder on her desk.

'When?' she asked. 'Where? … How long ago?'

Pauses elapsed in the stillness of the room. Moretti could tell by the questions she was asking that this was a new case. After a moment, she replaced the phone in its cradle. There was a minute's reflection before she turned to Moretti.

'I hope you haven't unpacked,' she said.

Chapter Seven

The arrivals terminal at Belfast airport was busy. Detective Boyle had told Nash where their transport would be waiting courtesy of the station. The only vehicle they could see, aside from taxis, was a 4x4 Nissan pick-up. It was two-tone in colour – white and rust – and attached to the back was a sheep trailer. The livestock chewed away and jostled each other for the best position next to the air slits in the trailer's side.

Leaning against the unit was a gangly-looking man. Nash put him at mid-forties, six foot with a good head of hair. Brown locks curled out from underneath the dark beanie he was wearing. He sported a pair of combat style trousers that had stains at the knees. From the smell, Nash surmised he'd fallen in sheep dung getting his flock into the trailer. A fur-lined brown corduroy bomber jacket, and plaid shirt completed the look. A few buttons were open at the neck and Nash noticed his pectoral muscles peeking out the top. Gangly he may have appeared, but he was lean and fit. The man's deep green eyes flashed at Nash, joined by a smile that revealed good teeth. He pushed himself away from the trailer, removing his beanie. He approached them both and stuffed the hat in his jacket pocket as he reached for their small luggage cases.

'Mornin', officers. I'll be taking you from here so jump in the truck but mind your heads as you get in,' he said.

Nash felt her cheeks flush. He took the small carry-on case she'd brought, lifting it with the care she imagined he'd handle a new-born lamb. Moretti insisted he'd manage his own, and the male shrugged in acceptance as he placed Nash's in the covered section of the pick-up on a blanket, she assumed, he'd laid out in anticipation.

Once they were in the cab of the pick-up the man introduced himself. His warm Northern Irish lilt was captivating to listen to.

'My name is William, but you can call me Will. Sit back and relax and I'll have you both at the farm in the blink of a ewe's eye,' he said, winking at Nash who was sat next to him.

Moretti, crunched against the passenger door, pursed his lips as he extracted his arm from the door handle that dug into his side.

It suddenly occurred to Nash that William could be mistaken and picked up the wrong people despite his initial greeting.

'Er… probably should have asked sooner but you do know who we are?' Nash said.

Will gunned the engine, and they all jolted as the trailer engaged with the tow bar.

'Sure I do – not many detectives from The Smoke waiting on a lift and fair play to you – you don't look like locals to me. My brother told me to look out for a man and a woman dressed like they were going to an office and looking lost. Well, I'd say you two fit the bill – so I do,' Will said, relaxing into his seat. He leant forward and caught Moretti's eye.

'Brother?' Moretti enquired.

'Eldest brother. DC Boyle, Pete Boyle, your woman here, spoke to,' he said. 'Push the cassette home will you.' Will nodded at the cassette player in the truck.

Moretti did as directed. The tape was collected by the machine. Moretti shut his eyes in anticipation of the music he was about to endure. To his surprise, the unmistakable drums of Buddy Rich entered the cab and after the initial intro they were soon joined by his big band. Trumpets streamed through the speakers and a lively dance hall jazz tune started up.

'I bet you thought it would be some traditional folk shite.' Will smiled and laughed.

Moretti returned the smile, and they all began to relax into the journey. They headed towards Omagh and the Sperrin mountains, some forty-seven kilometres from Belfast. A beautiful part of Northern Ireland full of rich history, countryside, valleys, and mountain ranges. Nash enjoyed glimpses of Belfast as truck and trailer moved through the streets.

Nash's gut was telling her this wasn't going to be anything like their Glasgow trip. DC Boyle had been insistent he'd arrange all their transport and accommodation. He was keen to prove that there were better places to spend the government's money than on overpriced hire cars and hotels, despite an agreed government rate for both. He'd assured her their accommodation would be comfortable, close to the scene, and he'd supply all the transport they'd need.

Will played the host well, pointing out various places of interest that cropped up along the route. He drove carefully and Nash considered this was due to the cargo he towed more than a desire to stick to the law of the road having two detectives in the front. Nash thought about where they'd be staying and rather than mull it over, she asked the question.

'Pete, Detective Boyle, explained that our accommodation would be close to the crime scene. He never said what the hotel's name was though?' Nash asked.

Will threw the pick-up left then right, avoiding a stray dog that had ventured onto the single-track road they were on. When he patted Nash's knee, it took her by surprise. It felt more like a pat of reassurance he'd give to a sheepdog than anything else. She decided to let it go this once.

'Sure now, you'll be close to the crime scene as Pete told you. No need to worry about a hotel, though. You'll be staying at Casa Boyle or High Peak Farm as it's known.'

Will nodded and Nash's eyes widened.

'Whoa, I did not agree to that,' she said, throwing Moretti a look that said she hadn't.

The offer of a lift had felt acceptable. DC Boyle had explained that a hire car would need to be a 4x4 to operate in the terrain they'd be in, and he'd offered to provide appropriate police transport. Nash was beginning to regret the haste with which she'd accepted the offer.

The call from DC Boyle had imparted similar information to that of DI Gordon's. DC Boyle had told her there had been a murder in Ireland, and the bullet had been a match to those found in Glasgow. He'd called DI Gordon who was too busy to get involved but had quickly offered Nash's number. Boyle didn't want any help and hadn't asked her to attend the scene. He was quite happy to send the ballistic report via a secure server, a recognised way of sharing confidential information between certain units knowing it would get to the right person.

According to Boyle, the shooting in Northern Ireland had occurred two days after the one in Scotland and had taken place in an area of remote open countryside. There was no CCTV, and it was too early for full forensics, aside from the bullet – a single shot to the back of the victim's head with no doubt it was the same gun involved.

Finally, the pick-up swung a right and bumped off the single-track road. They drove along a rugged dirt track that elevated towards a large farmhouse. Nash leant forward and looked through the windscreen. The clear blue sky was interrupted by wisps of cirrus cloud hovering above the tops of the surrounding hills. A buzzard drifted in the distance, its wing feathers flicked up like splayed fingers. Will noticed her interest.

'In a month, these hills will be covered in wildflowers and the lot in the back there will be birthing spring lambs,' he said, nodding proudly to himself as he spoke.

They arrived at a five-bar metal gate. Will sat back and jutted his chin at Nash. Moretti instinctively opened his door and dropped from his seat and began to walk towards the closed gate.

'Watch now,' Will said. He was smiling at Nash, and Nash couldn't understand his interest. Nash thought Moretti was acting perfectly reasonably as she didn't expect Will to have a remote gate opener and it was something the passenger in any police vehicle would be expected to do without question.

Will killed the engine. Through Moretti's opened door, Nash heard the unmistakable patter of what she thought were dog's paws followed by a ferocious yapping. Moretti began to back away as a Jack Russell terrier bounded towards him. The dog, all teeth and gums, was dragging a rope tied to his collar. Moretti had thought better of getting bitten and was at the truck when a *clang* of metal could be heard. Attached to the rope was a stick which was caught in the metal bars of the gate, preventing the dog from venturing beyond it. Moretti shook his head in disbelief.

'Come now, Nick, he'll be fine now he's seen me. You can open it no problem and I promise no further surprises are in store for you,' Will said.

Moretti walked towards the gate with a degree of caution. He opened the large metal barrier and stepped forwards. The dog ignored him and having backed up and released the stick from the metal he went to join Will and Nash.

Will walked back to the gate and closed it. He dropped the ramp to the trailer and Nash and Moretti watched as the sheep stepped down the steel and seemed to navigate towards the only other gate to a field that abutted the farmhouse, a majestic-looking red brick building that could appear in any TV production set in the countryside in the Edwardian era.

Will grabbed Nash and Moretti's cases and set them down.

'See that cottage over there,' Will said, pointing west at a pinprick of white against a section of green.

'I think so,' Nash said.

'That's where you'll both be staying. It's well stocked, so it is, courtesy of DC Boyle and me.' He smiled and nodded.

'How will we get there?' Moretti asked.

Will nodded at them both and they took the action as meaning they should follow him, which they did. They walked around the side of the house towards a stone barn. Will slid open a large wooden door and waved them in. Inside were two quad bikes. Will patted them both as though he were greeting old friends.

'I'll get some rope so you can strap your cases on the racks,' he said, leaving Nash and Moretti staring at the bikes.

Nash had to ask, 'Where is the crime scene? I couldn't see any scene tape or any police vehicle at all.'

Will rubbed at his brow before he rolled his shirtsleeves up his forearms, ready for work.

'You're sleeping in it,' he said, turning to walk away, leaving Moretti and Nash, mouths agape.

Moretti stared at the machine he'd decided was his.

'Priceless, just priceless. Wait until I tell the team about this,' he said, chuckling and shaking his head.

He looked at Nash whose skin had paled in shock. Her mouth felt dry, and she began to bite the inside of her cheeks. An action she hadn't done since she was a child.

'How in the hell did we end up here?' she asked.

Moretti looked at her. 'I have no idea,' he said, his eyes firmly set on Nash.

Chapter Eight

Will returned on his quad bike. His collie sat proudly on the rack at the rear. Nash and Moretti remained staring out at the countryside that surrounded them. Will turned off the engine and remained on his quad.

'You'll be wanting to get settled in, I imagine, so let's go and show you the cottage where you'll be staying,' he said. With a quick lesson in quad bike control, they readied to move off.

As Nash sat upon her machine, she felt conscious of the absence of a crash helmet but felt confident Will knew the land better than any of them and would choose a route that wouldn't be too hazardous for two southern detectives used only to bus, tube, and car.

Nash had ridden a motorbike at the earliest age she could take her test. Will spent some time showing Moretti what to do while Nash left hers ticking over.

Will mounted his bike, and they all set off, following his lead towards the white dot in the distance. Nash enjoyed rising and lowering herself in the seat as she navigated the vehicle over the undulating land. She could see Moretti had taken to it too. His face lit up like a child with a new toy. She was pleased he was getting the chance to kick back and relax away from London, or any city, for that matter. She knew he needed it. He rarely took leave. He preferred to be at work as much as she did. She couldn't fathom how he could steer while recording his journey on his phone, though.

As she negotiated a mound of earth, a scar her thigh twinged. It was from a knife wound. The result of an arrest at the culmination of a covert deployment. She sat back down and reduced her speed, but kept Will in sight. Will looked back at them; a shepherd herding his human flock. On the back of his bike, the black and white collie faced into the light breeze and appeared to be smiling as they rode.

Nash never thought she'd be exploring Northern Ireland in search of evidence and a new lead for her crime.

The whitewashed stone of the cottage became evident, and Will sat back on the quad as he observed his land. A grey flat cap had replaced the beanie and his hair billowed out from under it.

Will slowed his bike, letting Nash and Moretti catch him up. He indicated with a sweep of his arm they should follow in a single file formation, and it was good that he did. They'd hit a track that was banked either side by gorse bushes and Nash felt relieved she was putting her biker's coat to appropriate use.

The track led them to the front of the stone-built cottage. An area of hard standing had been created from shingle as a result of quarry blasting. Nash noticed an off-road pick-up truck parked outside. The door to the cottage was open. They killed their engines once the bikes were lined up and got off.

'Well, now, I hope it suits you both,' Will announced, striding into the cottage with Nash's case in hand having deftly untethered it from the rear pannier rack of her quad.

Nash certainly felt taken care of. She was hesitant to step inside after what Will had said about the crime scene, but it was a futile precaution as there was clearly someone in there already. As they stepped in, Nash was met by an older version of Will. A pistol hanging from a body-worn holster attracted her eye. This was no farmer.

DC Pete Boyle held out his hand to Nash as Moretti put his phone away. Boyle greeted them both like they were family. A table in a small kitchen area had been laid with cold cuts of meat and a salad in rustic pottery dishes.

'Thought you'd be hungry after your trip and God knows there's nowhere to eat but the farm in these parts,' DC Boyle said. With a scrape of his chair, he motioned for them all to be seated. Once they settled, DC Boyle produced a folder and handed it to Nash.

'It's all in there. Photos of the scene and the ballistic report,' he said.

Nash looked at him and didn't open the folder.

'Where's my scene,' she said, leaning back while she waited and for him to reply.

DC Boyle chewed and swallowed.

'Now then, Pip, it's not *your* scene, it's mine. I figured as I've done everything that can be done, you'd appreciate eating before I took you to see it. You're not in Glasgow now.' He smirked with a flick of his eyes at his brother.

Nash now knew that DC Boyle had discovered more than he'd let on from his *brief* conversation with DI Gordon. DC Boyle wasn't finished.

'I bet you weren't a thief-taker in your time, Pippa,' he said, shaking the saltcellar over his food as though he had an excess to get rid of.

'What's that supposed to mean?' Nash asked.

'You take no prisoners, that's for certain. Much like our mam, hey Willy?' he remarked as he smirked and chewed on a section of ham before pointing at her with a fork.

'We do things differently here as you'll become aware but that doesn't mean we aren't professional. Now, to answer your question, once you've finished the food, I'll take you to the scene. It's very close by,' he said.

The food finished, they left the cottage and followed DC Boyle along a rough shingle path towards a mound of coarse grass. Nash was becoming irritated at the slow approach. While she appreciated the hospitality, she wasn't a tourist and didn't wish to be treated like one.

They circumnavigated the mound of grass and as Nash and Moretti breached the corner, they were met by a small drain hole in the earth. A large metal cover lay discarded next to it and DC Boyle was disappearing below ground thanks to a metal ladder that dipped just below the surface of the soil. Boyle looked up at her.

'Come on now, your ladyship, *your* scene awaits,' Boyle said.

Nash observed the top of his head dip further into the concrete tube. She looked at Moretti who shrugged, then she placed a foot on the rung of the ladder and followed Boyle down below ground.

Moretti followed Nash, and Will remained above ground. Boyle flicked a toggle style switch attached to the concrete walls. Lights illuminated around them and Boyle pulled open a thick internal security door. It was as though they'd stepped back in time. Nash let her eyes adjust to the artificial light as further overhead lamps picked out a cavern of concrete. Metal shelving lined the bare grey walls. A distinctive smell took her straight back to Glasgow and the gangly-looking youth they'd passed at the strip of shops. The smell of cannabis was overpowering. It was as though they'd opened the drugs safe in the custody area after a fresh seizure but on a much larger scale.

'I see you recognise the smell of illegal horticulture,' Boyle remarked.

Nash pulled up the scarf she was wearing across her nose. Moretti inhaled like it was his last breath.

Boyle nodded that they should follow him, and they did. A corridor now linked them to a series of smaller rooms. As they approached one near the end, she could see a bank of CCTV monitors. Boyle flicked them on. They showed the inside of the bunker only. Nash found that odd; the idea that whoever had set this up was not interested to monitor the area around the bunker troubled her.

'What was this place before it became a grow house?' she asked.

'It was an old bunker from the Cold War era, for those of us left if the big red button was pressed. Why my dad agreed to have it put below his land, I do not know. I'd hazard a guess it was about money, but he never said. We were young, and it was fascinating to play here. There was already a smaller bunker used during the Second World War but it was updated and extended,' Boyle replied.

'So what happened here?' Nash asked, keen to move on from the history lesson and focus on the reason they were there.

Boyle waved them into another room opposite where they were. The door was open. He flicked on a light. On the floor was a dark patch in contrast with the wash of grey concrete. Nash could see the shade was dried blood. She opened the folder she'd brought down. The image on the top page showed a mattress within the room they were in. An item no longer present. The mattress in the image was against the wall, and the body of a Vietnamese male was sprawled next to it. His hands and feet hog-tied with rope. What would have been the victim's head was decorating the concrete wall. The blood spatter pattern Nash had seen before. The sign of someone shot at close range. Very close range. DC Boyle leant over her shoulder and tapped the picture with his index finger.

'He was kneeling when he was shot in the head. We have powder residue off his hair. I have to say, in all my years, I've seen nothing like it before,' he said.

Nash let her eyes take in the room. The walls were stark and what would have been a sleeping area devoid of warmth. It was a cell. In fact, a cell had more comforts than this. Toilet facilities consisted of a bucket. There was a room with a shower that didn't work and a kitchen area that consisted of a fridge-freezer, single hotplate, and a microwave.

'How many people were down here and why on earth did you not know what was going on?' she said to Boyle who pursed his lips.

'I've asked myself the same thing, Pip. I've asked Will too as, technically, the farm and cottage are his to manage, but in truth it was happening under our noses,' he said. He left the room and Nash and Moretti followed him into the main arena.

'That's not good enough,' Nash said, her arms crossed as she hugged the folder.

'I know... how can a cannabis farm be right under our feet? It's a question I'm desperately embarrassed about. Will let the cottage to a man who claimed to be from your part of the world. Fella gave his name as John Symes and all his details checked out. Symes said he was a writer. He wasn't published but wanted a place he could escape to. He paid a year's rent up front as he needed the freedom to come and go as he pleased, he'd said. I checked the details myself and they all seemed legitimate, so they did. The money arrived when he said it would and Will met the guy here and gave him the keys.' Boyle swallowed and looked at the floor.

'So how were you paid? There must be financial records that can be traced to find this man and where his funds are coming and going,' Nash asked, but she already knew the answer. She just needed to hear it from Boyle.

Boyle paced the floor and let out a sigh.

Nash noticed that her stomach had begun to tighten. She glanced at Boyle's gun that hung from the sling holster. They were in the middle of nowhere, underground, at a murder site where a man had been shot and by all accounts no one heard anything. Boyle stopped pacing and faced them both. His hands at rest on top of his head, fingers clasped together. He screwed his face up before he spoke.

'He paid cash,' he said, and let his hands flop by his side.

'I wasn't here when the transaction took place. Will could see nothing wrong with it. It happens in farming, especially out here. We pay our taxes, but times are hard and – fuck,' he exclaimed.

Nash could see he was fearful of the investigation leading back to his brother, but that wasn't Nash's problem.

'Why are you assigned to investigate this? It's a bit close, isn't it?' she asked.

Boyle laughed.

'Pip, we're not like the Met. We don't have that many detectives. I'm it, aside from a couple of others at the station, but they all know me. We grew up together, went to school together. We're practically family. It doesn't matter whether it's me or them. Truth be told, I'll do all I can to discover who killed the poor fella, even if that brings my brother into it for the stupidity with the money,' he said.

Nash said nothing. She was too busy taking in the deprivation the young Vietnamese male must have endured. How did he get here? When? Why wasn't he ever seen? She wondered where the main power source was to the bunker. A cannabis farm needed light, heat, and water to operate quickly and efficiently. Nash felt DC Boyle was reading her mind as he moved them to another room. Against a wall stood an oil-powered generator and a ventilation system in place that Nash hadn't noticed was running, but it suddenly occurred to her they were deep underground and air had to be pumped in from somewhere.

'Who put the generator down here?' she asked, as she moved a few overhead lamps that hadn't been seized as evidence.

DC Boyle was relaxed as he spoke. 'The electric has always been here, as has cold water. As for the generator, that must have been lowered down the entranceway. Whoever was running this place didn't want to be found, that's for certain. The only other place they could've got power from was the farm, and Will would've been the first to see his electric bill go through the roof. The farm uses a fair amount of power to run but not being dairy, the costs aren't as high by comparison. What I'm saying is, he'd have seen if they'd tapped into the farm grid. They'd have to run a cable all the way from the pole down here and he's out every day and would've noticed,' he said, scratching his temple.

'Do you need to see anything else?' he asked.

Nash shook her head. She'd seen enough.

'One last thing,' she said.

Boyle raised his eyes in anticipation of the question. 'Go on.'

'What state was the crop in when the body was discovered?' she asked.

'It was harvested. Just the trays and lamps were left,' Boyle said.

Nash nodded. 'You said on the phone that Will found the body?' she asked.

'Technically,' Boyle replied, raising his eyebrows.

Nash looked up at the ceiling and then at Boyle.

'Go on,' she said.

Boyle rubbed his chin and looked out the corner of his eye.

'Look, he was out rounding up sheep and found he was short by one. He's not the type of guy to come back in and not bother looking so he came down here to see of one had bounded the dry-stone wall and got into the field above us.' He paused. 'As he got close, he saw the hatch was off. It's unusual, as it's always shut. He doesn't want an animal falling down it. He assumed his sheep had done just that. He climbed down and found the place had been used. He got jumpy and called me. I came over and did a proper search. I found the Vietnamese fella in the room. That's the technical part and I've recorded that in my statement which is back at the station.'

Nash didn't reply. It was clear that once the cottage had been let Will had nothing more to do with it, unless asked.

Chapter Nine

A howling wind swirled around the white stone brick of the cottage. Moretti had got the fire going, and it was ablaze. Years of doing the same on his boat had paid off. That and all the equipment they'd been supplied by DC Boyle and Will made the job easier. There'd been talk of going to the pub, but the weather had turned nasty and they'd all decided that staying put would be the best thing for the evening. A storm was forecast, and no one needed to be outside.

DC Boyle had said he was needed on nights and had left them after they'd exit the bunker. Moretti had taken timeout to partake of some shooting; firing Boyle's gun. Boyle had erected some targets and set them against a quarry wall. Moretti had never fired a gun, but Boyle told him he was a natural with the pistol and that had made Moretti very pleased as he'd always had a hankering for joining the firearms command but then he'd become a detective and set that aside. There were armed detective roles, and he now felt that could be a realistic move.

While Moretti played guns, Nash was back at the cottage where she'd laid out the contents of the folder DC Boyle had handed over. A collage of images of the scene covered the wooden surface of the farmhouse table. They stayed there until Moretti had returned and Boyle had left.

It was evening now, and Nash had taken a break from work and prepared herself a meal with the leftovers from lunch. Moretti had helped himself to a bottle of Scotch he'd carried from the airport. They had another bottle they'd give to Boyle when they saw him at the police station in the morning.

Nash sat against the arm of the worn sofa and sipped her drink. Moretti had made them both an Irish coffee, and she was enjoying the end of what had been a challenging day. Despite the scene visit being brief, she'd struggled with the solitude of the environment. She couldn't calm her mind. It was churning over with images of the bunker, the playground in Glasgow, and her own scene from three years ago. She'd tried to dial her inside team. No signal. The pending storm meant she'd no choice but to remain at the cottage. Boyle had said the farm's phone was down. It would have to wait until the morning when they visited Boyle's station.

There was a knock at the cottage's door, and it was burst open by a gust of wind. Nash got up from her seat and braced herself for the intruder. They heard the stomp of feet and then the sound of someone coughing. It was DC Boyle. Boyle entered the living room dressed in a pair of jeans and a crisp white linen shirt.

'I got cover for tonight, so I have, and the weather's easing off. So – how's about I take you out for the night and show you some traditional nightlife? A spot of folk music and plenty of drink and craic,' he said, clapping his hands together. His eyes darted between Nash and Moretti. He reminded Nash of a child trying to get his mates to come out to play. Moretti didn't need asking twice and was on his feet and conducting a pat down of his pockets stopping once he'd located his wallet and warrant card.

Nash shook her head. 'I'm good thanks. Enjoy yourselves and I'll see you tomorrow.'

Moretti dumped his warrant card on the table and left with Boyle.

Nash relaxed now she had the place to herself. She didn't mind Moretti's company – she enjoyed it – but there was nothing she enjoyed more than her own space. Time for her to think. She showered and changed into yoga trousers she loved to train and relax in. She walked into the kitchen and finished towelling her hair. She left the lounge door open and the heat from the fire filtered through the small space.

She topped up her drink and revisited the images of the scene. The victim was a Vietnamese male in his early twenties. At this stage of Boyle's enquiry, he was unidentified. Boyd had started his own enquiries with Interpol to try to ascertain his identity. Was he a victim of human trafficking or had he been in the country a while and been sent to manage the cannabis plants? Boyd had told Nash that the victim had been fingerprinted by police under the supervision of a pathologist. A DNA sample had been taken, and all had been submitted to the appropriate authorities for searches.

It was common knowledge that people were trafficked to work on cannabis farms, but Nash wondered why Boyd hadn't made progress with establishing any leads in that area? How did Will not know that this man was on his land? Will must have seen the guy at some point? Maybe the victim stayed below ground for the entire time they were here? The thought of the poor soul kept alive within his own tomb made her shudder. Nash knew that once you were in the bunker communication was cut off. Communication – how would the victim have communicated to the outside world if anything was wrong or when the cannabis was ready? Maybe he wasn't meant to. Maybe he was left there for the time it would take the cannabis to grow for harvest before any contact was made. But how would he feed himself?

She sipped her drink, looked at the glass, and drained it. Images of the contorted and bloodied corpse littered the table. She pulled a photo towards her and studied it. Boyle had said that the victim was hog-tied and shot in the head at close range. From what Nash was seeing, that didn't fit. It didn't fit because she could see that the victim's legs appeared broken. How on earth could someone who lived below ground break both their legs? There was nowhere to fall other than off the ladder on the descent. Even if the victim had slipped a rung, she doubted the drop would be enough to cause that considerable amount of trauma. Something stank. It wasn't the stale smell of the bunker that had clung to her clothing. Boyle had also been the one to take the scene photos. She looked at the bottle of Scotch. They'd made a good dent in it before Moretti had left with Boyle. She considered she may have had too much of it, and that was affecting her thought process.

She was tired. Tired through endless hours of work.

She gathered up the photos and stuffed them back in the folder as best she could. Her judgment was clouded, and this was one reason why she rarely drank. She had chosen to on this occasion as she was out in the middle of nowhere and it was highly unlikely that she'd be called upon to deal with anything. She could relax for once. She took the bottle and glass and as she passed the cottage door, she paused; Moretti had a key. She locked the door from the inside and took the key from the hole. She took everything through to the bedroom where she shut the door. The room was swirling as she gently lay back on the sprung mattress of her bed.

She set the bottle and glass on a bedside table and placed her forearm over her eyes. The mattress embraced her body as her svelte frame sank into the springs.

Tears prickled in the corners of her eyes. A rare feeling. Her mind fought the release of emotions that had become pent-up from too many years of trying to be the best she could be for everyone. A punishment that afflicted a detective who was as passionate and dedicated to their job as she was. In the womb-like sanctuary of her room, she sobbed as she let the angst expel from her body.

* * *

The darkness of the previous evening's storm had given way to a clear start. Nash was awoken by the sounds of sheep braying. She had fallen asleep in her clothes, and she suspected it might be colder here than in London. Her head felt good and there were no residual feelings from alcohol or emotions, which was a blessing. She checked her watch, and the time showed 6 a.m. She grabbed her running shoes and put them on. Her tongue felt dry, as did her throat. She got up and walked through to the kitchen mindful not to awaken Moretti. A glass of water revived her body, which thanked her by jolting her synapses awake as the cool liquid coursed through her alcohol-riddled body.

She tiptoed quietly towards Moretti's room to check on him. Why? She didn't know, but she hadn't heard him return last night. She had been in a deep alcoholic haze though, so she suspected that was the reason. The door to Moretti's room was ajar. As she placed her hands against the oak of the door, she eased it open and peered in. His bed was empty. The bedding untouched. She made the decision to check the rest of the cottage, calling out Moretti's name as she moved. Nothing. Knowing Moretti, she assumed he had made other sleeping arrangements.

She walked back to the kitchen and looked in the fridge. The brown paper-wrapped parcel of sausages and bacon would do her good on her return from a run.

She grabbed the cottage key and opened the locked front door.

Something was preventing it from opening. A low groan emanated from the outside as the base of the door connected with what was obviously human. Human and male. Nash shouldered the door and Moretti let out a harsh moan. Nash shifted his body along the shingle, using the door as leverage. He muttered, 'stop', as she pushed enough to step through the gap.

Chapter Ten

'Nick, Nick, what on earth's happened to you?' she asked.

Nash crouched down by his side and felt his pulse. It was as she expected. Not strong, but not of any major concern. From the smell of alcohol that arose from him, she had an idea of the affliction he was enduring. Mixed in with the stale smell of beer and whisky was a heady odour of sheep manure that wasn't coming from anywhere else but him. She leant back, leaving him in the foetal position covered in a thin grey blanket. She lifted the blanket to check he wasn't in need of an ambulance and discovered he was dressed in a set of farming waterproofs and a reflective vest. Nash shook her head as Moretti gradually sat up on his hands. His hair caked in dirt to match his clothes.

'Morning, ma'am,' he offered in a mutter, as he pinched his eyes against the weak sun.

Moretti's resurrection was interrupted by the sound of a quad bike's engine that was getting louder from behind them. Will appeared through the gate to the cottage astride his machine and killed the engine as he got off the bike. He removed his flat hat and waved it about his face as he got closer.

'Now then, Nicholas. Glad you're alive so I am,' he said, smiling down at Moretti.

Nash stood up, and they helped Moretti to his feet.

'What in the hell was he doing outside all night? He could have died out here,' Nash exclaimed to Will.

They helped Moretti into the living room. Will got the fire going and Nash grabbed her duvet cover and dumped it on the moribund Moretti who sat in a seat next to the fire. His shoulders juddered. Will looked up at Nash and stood away from the flames.

'Pete was right about you, Pip, you have the look of our ma before she'd fire off a salvo and destroy the craic,' he said, shifting on his feet like a boxer his cap over his crotch.

Moretti coughed. 'It's my fault, Pip. I couldn't hang on to the bike to get back here. Will had to roll me down the hill and thought it better if I wear the waterproofs he carried and the yellow vest so he could see me, as I... well – as it was pitch-black,' he offered, with a crease at his mouth. He finished and rubbed the back of his head. He grimaced and flinched as his fingers hit a lump.

She never expected Moretti to act like a monk, but this was a step up in alcoholic oblivion even for him. She was beginning to think he might have a problem. She considered how much of the whisky she'd got through last night when Moretti had left before she'd collapsed on the bed, room swirling. At least he hadn't died of hypothermia. She walked away from them both and went into the kitchen where she set the kettle to boil.

As she stood at the sink, she began to relax. Will and Moretti talked in hushed tones like a couple of teenagers caught smoking by their mother. She was glad there'd been no harm done. They had a long day ahead, and she had no intention of staying here another night. She brought a round of teas back in and their voices subsided.

'I'm off for a run. There's enough hot water for a shower, Nick, I suggest you take one but don't use it all,' she said.

Nash stepped back outside and turned out of the drive. She hurdled a turnstile and set off towards the hill in front of the cottage. A vast expanse of nature emerged from hidden depths. She'd not bothered with a warmup. She'd done enough dips and stretches getting Moretti to his feet. The light morning breeze felt cool against her skin, which began to expel the previous night's poison as she moved. The damp heath sank gently under her feet. She made reasonable time and breached the penultimate summit of earth, slowing to a walk. The wind was strong, and she knew she'd have to watch her footing.

She dipped at the waist and rested her hands upon her knees. As her breathing settled, she looked below at the cottage. From her vantage point, she could see the lie of the land and where the bunker sat within it. There was no access to the bunker other than the farm road. With the metal cover in place, the land appeared to consume the murder site. She could make out the entrance to the bunker from where she was, but she'd ran past it, as it wasn't clear from below despite having been to the location the day before. You'd have to either know the history of the land, know where to look, or see it from the air to have any idea it existed. There was no tank that she could see which might contain fuel to power the generator. She hadn't seen any fuel tank below ground either, but she hadn't been looking for that at the time. It wasn't her investigation, and Boyle had been very clear about that. She was a detective though, and questions arose as naturally as the sun.

As the questions cropped up, she raised her head. The land sprawled out before her towards the horizon. Will's place was the only farm property she could see for miles.

He could've been on the other side of the hills and never have known anyone was driving down to the farmhouse. She felt glad the job wasn't hers because it looked a mess. Boyle had said he had the bullet back at the station that was taken from the victim's skull. It was locked in an exhibits store, and she could see it if she wished but she wouldn't be able to take it with her at this time.

Her body was cooling rapidly so she began her zigzagged descent back towards the cottage.

* * *

Nash showered and changed while the kettle boiled. She dressed for a day of travel in a pair of dark denim jeans, a black T-shirt finished off with a brown leather belt. She dispensed with drying her hair, opting to tie it back in a ponytail. She grabbed her fresh brew of tea and they all ate the breakfast Will had prepared. He'd timed it to be ready. He'd seen her descending the hillside and accounted for her getting showered. A trick his mother had taught him; she'd done the same for him when she watched him tend the sheep first thing before coming home in the morning.

When their mother passed away, everything had been left to Will and DC Boyle. Will, being the farmer, had the job of day-to-day management with Boyle as a sleeping partner. Will had described his brother as being the kind of sleeping partner who only awoke when the shit hit the fan. He told them over breakfast that he hadn't seen his brother in a while, as he'd been so busy with work.

Will dropped them both at the police station. A tired-looking building and certainly not what Nash or Moretti had expected.

'Morning, all,' Boyle said, striding across the station yard to greet them.

Will informed his brother he'd be back in an hour to take them to the airport and left. The yard was devoid of any marked police car. Nash clocked the familiar shape of a powerful motorbike in a covered garage area, wrapped under a waterproof cover. There were a couple of nondescript cars the detectives used for work too. As she looked at the police building, she felt as though she'd stepped back in time.

Nash went into the Intelligence office, the walls adorned with black and white signed images of legendary jazz drummers. On a single cabinet a portable cassette player played a jazz compilation.

Never in Nash's service had she visited a station that couldn't be further from a police environment. There was nothing to suggest this room contained any intelligence about anything. She made up her mind to keep the visit as brief as she could muster. DC Boyle unlocked the exhibits cupboard that looked more like one the cleaner would use. DC Boyle rummaged in the cupboard, then came out.

'The exhibits must have been collected and be on the way to central stores,' Boyle announced.

Nash let out a long sigh. She'd hoped to see the bullet rather than the photos and also the victim's clothing and anything else DC Boyle had gathered. It wasn't to be.

'Sorry, Pip. We don't have much space, so the quicker it's out the easier it is for us,' Boyle offered by way of a reasonable explanation.

The atmosphere was further polluted by the smell of cigars. A foul aftershave followed the scent of tobacco as a fifty-something male entered the room carrying a coffee mug in one hand and a cigar in the other. Boyle straightened in posture as the male entered. The man wasn't particularly large in height or build. He was wearing a pair of dark grey flannel trousers, a white shirt and a cardigan. On his belt was a pistol holster. By the pristine look of the leather, it had been strapped to him for Nash and Moretti's benefit only. He had greying hair swept into a quiff and his forearms sported faded black ink from what appeared to be an anchor tattoo.

'DI Nash, this is DI John Flanagan, or John Boy as we know him,' Boyle said with a mock salute.

Flanagan gave a short smile and shook hands with Nash and Moretti.

'Pete, a word in my office, please,' Flanagan said, excusing himself from the room.

Nash took the opportunity to speak with Moretti. She leant into his side and spoke in hushed tones while Moretti stared up at a poster for an upcoming outdoor jazz festival.

'We need to leave. This place is beyond a joke and stinks of an old boys' smoking club that's got out of hand,' she said.

Moretti nodded in agreement, and Nash was pleased to see the colour had returned to his pallid cheeks.

From what she could ascertain, they were in the incident room. Boyle and Flanagan were the team. Boyle had spoken of another detective, and Nash hoped he or she was out on enquiries. She made a mental note that whenever her team appeared to be stepping off the accelerator pedal, she should think back to this and laugh it off.

Boyle returned and Nash recognised the look of a DC who'd just been given a dressing down. There'd been no raised words. Flanagan's office was on the same floor, and there were only two to the building.

'I'm to go out and detect. I've called Will and he'll be with you shortly,' Boyle said, motioning with his hand towards the door.

It was time to leave. Moretti said his farewells, as did Nash who was less enthusiastic. Will was outside by the time they stepped out of the building. Moretti went to his case and retrieved the bottle of Scotch they'd bought from duty free on the way out. He handed it to Boyle and returned to the truck.

Will had dropped back to talk with his brother and had now returned. He got in and they set off for the airport.

Chapter Eleven

They'd been travelling for many hours and Nash didn't feel mentally fresh enough to face the main office. She'd called in, by phone, before they'd boarded the flight. All was in hand according to Owen Matthews whom she'd designated as her acting DI while she was away. She'd made good use of the brief downtime at home and was now back in her office bright and early the following day ready to meet and greet her team and get them up to speed on what was known. There was an email on the internal system from DS Carl Harris of the undercover unit. She read through the contents marked for her eyes only and made some notes in her phone before shutting it down. She tapped the screen of the iPhone with her fingernail as she contemplated the directive the message had contained.

The voices of her team soon drifted along the corridor. Voices of laughter. Two she recognised – Jonesy and Owen Matthews – shortly followed by the booming yawn and assured steps of JJ. She smiled as she flicked through the paperwork on her desk. She was home. The trailing geranium had perked up as the first hit of water reached the roots. She gathered the documents she needed and entered the main incident room. There was the usual stifled round of *good mornings* as her team settled in.

She did the rounds of the room and, satisfied everyone was in good form, gave them a five-minute warning of attendance in the briefing room. As she entered the briefing room, Owen Matthews was already setting up the projector screen.

'Morning, ma'am,' he said, tapping various keys on the computer.

Nash sat down.

'Any issues while I was away, Owen?' she asked.

Owen sat down with a mug of coffee.

'Nothing – all very steady,' he said.

Squad members filed into the room. Nash watched as they all took their seats and Moretti joined her.

'Right, I'm sure you've all been very busy while I've been away.' Nash paused, while a few laughed and coughed.

Moretti leant forwards and pressed the keyboard for the first slide. An image of the Vietnamese victim appeared on screen. The room's chatter subsided to a hushed silence. Nash began.

'This is the victim from Northern Ireland. As you can see from this slide, he was executed by a single shot to the head. The victim's legs were also broken,' she said, circling a laser pointer at the victim's lower body on the slide.

'The murder scene was below ground in a disused bunker,' she continued. 'The bunker had been turned into a grow house for cannabis. The crop was gone by the time the body was discovered. The bullet taken from the victim was a match to the gun used in our murder as well as the one in Glasgow. Our gun is on the move. Where it will end up next is anyone's guess. What do we know from our own enquires? I appreciate I only made contact yesterday afternoon, but there was no phone signal in the area we were in. Trust me when I say there was little point in trying to use a phone at the police station.' Nash raised her eyebrows.

DS Matthews was the first to speak.

'We, as in my Intel desk, worked up what we could on the limited information we had. We've initiated enquiries with the shipping authorities to ascertain if any motorbikes similar to the one seen in Glasgow have travelled by boat. It's a long shot, pardon the pun, but we need to see if the bike was used in both shooting incidents. Where the bike is, the gun may be, and that's what we need to recover for our own investigation. I'm not suggesting that *if* we find the bike, we definitely find the gun. But I felt the enquiry needed running,' Matthews said.

There was no disagreement, and Nash nodded her approval at his decision.

'What about the CCTV from Glasgow? Any joy finding out more about the bike or the suspects?' Nash asked.

Matthews continued, 'The image has been enhanced and the make of the bike would appear to be a Kawasaki and certainly above a 250 cc engine. We don't have any index number. The one in Glasgow was a road bike and by the shape on CCTV, a sports model. The passenger sat higher than the rider. I think this was by design. So he could shoot above the driver's head if he couldn't approach the victim side on.'

Nash made a note in her daybook. It was a good observation.

'Any more on the gun?' Nash asked.

JJ was the one to speak now as he'd picked up that side of the enquiry.

'I've asked the source unit to speak with their friendlies, and DS Dillon has said he'll talk with their covert management unit about a separate reward for any information that leads to the gun's recovery. He's hoping it will be a significant amount, but he's making no promises. I've left a message for DC Boyle. I need to ascertain where the central exhibits store is over there so we can access the bullet from their scene if we need it for trial or our own forensic work. I've done the same with DI Gordon in Glasgow. I've secured all the exhibits from the Whittaker murder and they're all in our storage here. I'll keep on at the source unit, as really, they're our main hope of someone coming forward. We all know how quickly news on serious and organised crime travels. Maybe they'll hear something about where the gun is,' JJ said.

Nash sat back. She felt frustrated that she was reliant on outside forces to provide her the information she required and contacts she needed. Distance was an issue when you couldn't doorstep people and demand, with a degree of respect, what you required. The forces knew it too, hence the "I'll get back to you" approach or just failing to respond. She dismissed the negative chatter from her mind and continued.

'I want Interpol contacted. I need to know who this Vietnamese victim is and all we can about him. When did he arrive in the UK and how? Where was he staying before going underground and who is the mystery male who paid cash for the cottage hire? Before you, George, start up with *it's not for us to do* – it is. I need to know if our victims are connected. George – get the actions allocated. Let's find the gun, the bike, and whoever the hell is involved with these murders. Trust me when I tell you that no person deserves to die the way these men did.'

With that she stood up and the meeting came to a close.

Chapter Twelve

Moretti leant against the exterior wall of the police building. The sky was as grey as the smoke plumes he blew into it. He looked at his mobile. No messages. He'd tried DC Boyle and DI Gordon and there was nothing by way of reply. He'd spoken to Sagona and requested all enquiries with Scotland and Northern Ireland that pertained to the bullets and the victims be given to him. He was beginning to think DC Boyle and DI Gordon were ignoring him. He'd left messages on their phones and at their respective stations. He took a draw on his pipe and savoured the whisky and plum mix that occupied the bowl of the short-stemmed Savinelli briar.

As he inhaled, he thought about what Nash had said about Boyle and how she didn't trust him. Moretti thought back to what he could remember of the night out at the pub, in the village closest to the farm, and he'd wondered why Boyle had only remained for a few drinks, then made excuses and left him with Will. Not a way to treat a guest from an outside force.

Moretti wondered if Boyle had decided he was cut from the same cloth as Nash, hence leaving him with a farmer. Moretti thought the police station was a man den and nothing more. What did Nash expect when the station was occupied by blokes of a certain generation of policing?

Moretti's phone rang. He looked at the screen. It was a Glasgow area code, but not from a number he knew. He answered it.

'Hello?' he said, nodding at JJ who was leaving the building striding towards his car.

There was silence at the end of the phone. Moretti moved the screen from his ear and looked at it. It was still connected. There was a rustle on the line as though the phone was in someone's pocket but then a voice came on, it was PC McLachlan. Her voice sounded as though she'd completed a run.

'Nick, it's Kelly from Scotland,' she said.

'Hello, stranger, how's things up north?' Moretti said, moving away from the building to a green area where conversation wouldn't be overheard from an open office window.

'Can you talk?' she asked.

Moretti rubbed his chin. What on earth could this be about, he thought.

'Yes, of course, what's wrong?' he asked.

McLachlan steadied her voice, and the muted sounds of traffic indicated to Moretti she was in a call box.

'I'm in a public call box. I don't have long, but I really think you need to know that something's not right about the murder here,' she said.

Moretti remained silent and let her have the floor. She'd said she was pressed for time, so he hoped she'd speak freely and impart what she needed to quickly.

'The guy who would give me bits and pieces of street talk, well he's gone, vanished. It's totally out of character. He was as much a part of the estate as I am, without living on it. DI Gordon thinks it's great the wee man has done one. I'm not so sure though… as he… well, he told me he knew who'd done the shooting,' she said.

'Who?' Moretti asked, conscious of getting a name before her time ran out.

'Well, this is the thing, he never gave me a name. He wanted to meet me and not say over the phone. He said I should be alone and not with Gordon. He was supposed to meet me a few days ago, but he never turned up. I have to go but I just wanted to let you know that someone knew who'd done it, but now he's gone. I'm calling from this number, as DI Gordon didn't want me contacting you about anything. He said he wanted to handle all out of force contact, but I couldn't leave this to him,' she said. The line went dead.

Moretti made a screenshot of the call box number and the time the call was made and stored the information in a folder on his phone. He wiped the call history. He tapped out the remaining tobacco and entered the building. He took a sharp left and entered the corridor to the ground floor. The floor occupied by the Homicide Task Force and the Source Unit. He got to the plain door of the source unit and knocked. The person he hoped to find, the Silverfox, answered it. The Silverfox let him in and Moretti drew up a seat and sat next to the handler. The Silverfox leant back from Moretti in his own chair as he spoke.

'You always assume your work is of more importance and urgency than mine, don't you?' he said with a smirk, dimming his computer screen. He shuffled a set of contact sheets aside so Moretti couldn't read them and showed his palms to him. A sign that he had Moretti's attention.

'I know I can be a pain in the arse, but this is urgent,' Moretti said.

'Have you run it by Nash and George?' the handler asked, knowing full well what the answer would be.

'Er… no. But I will as soon as I have something,' Moretti said, his head cocked to the side.

The handler sighed and Moretti continued.

'Do you have any contacts in Northern Ireland or Glasgow that could conduct a confidential enquiry?' he asked.

Behind them a fish tank bubbled away and the soothing play of the water against the tank provided a calm ambience to the room. The Silverfox raised his eyebrows.

'International crime… interesting… interesting – and you're not talking to Nash… because?' he asked, knowing Moretti would be backed into a corner where he'd have to divulge why if he was to get the handler on his side.

'Look, do you run everything past your controller? I can't remember his name but he's a DI and I bet you don't tell him everything,' Moretti said, with a glint of playfulness in his eyes.

The Silverfox laughed. 'That's an outrageous allegation, DS Moretti,' he said with a smile.

Moretti laughed. 'I need to manage this myself. Nothing more than that,' Moretti said.

The handler got up and poured them both a coffee and they adjourned to an area of the office much like Nash's that had a couple of seats and a coffee table. A new addition thanks to the HTF leaving their office door open once.

'What do you need?' the handler asked.

Moretti took a deep breath before he began. He knew the train he was about to depart on could take him to a destination he wouldn't wish to get to, but he felt he had to go with his hunch.

'When Nash and I were in Northern Ireland, we came across a fella called DC Pete Boyle. Let's just say he was as maverick as they come, but he's triggered Nash's interest and that's never a good thing.' He paused while the handler laughed. They both knew that coming under Nash's radar was never a good call.

'So what do you need? I'll level with you. We have very little to do with anyone outside of London. I do have some contacts in Scotland but not Northern Ireland,' the Silverfox said.

Moretti nodded.

'Well, as it happens, Scotland might be the best place to start,' Moretti said.

The handler's eyes now screwed in confusion.

'What on earth are you investigating? I've not seen anything about a new murder your team has picked up,' the Silverfox said.

'This isn't new. It's a cold case, the Whittaker murder. Bullets from the gun used to kill Whittaker have surfaced in Scotland and Northern Ireland. We're trying to see if we can get ahead of anyone else and have first dibs at anyone arrested before they clam up and we get nowhere with charges that will hold in court.'

The Silverfox nodded his understanding. Moretti explained about the call from PC McLachlan and provided the handler with the number of the call box she'd used.

'There's not much to go on. A junky she used to talk to has gone on the trot, and you've no name for them. You're not using me to make contact with an old flame I hope!' the handler said. Tears of laughter arose in his wise eyes.

Moretti shook his head but admired the way the handler's mind worked. There weren't many left like him in the service. He was renowned in the covert world as one person a source would struggle to lie to as he always got the truth from them.

'I'd never do that, and she's not an old flame. Barely a spark,' Moretti said, as the handler got up to answer one of the four mobile phones that lay on his desk.

'I'm the only one here at the moment,' the Silverfox said, pointing at the array of communication he was responsible for. 'Leave and sickness have taken their toll.'

Moretti left him free to talk. He closed the door behind him and waited until the re-enforced door clicked home and sealed the detective inside.

Moretti knew that if things went sour, then Nash wouldn't be pleased. That was an understatement – she'd be livid. It wasn't the first time he'd acted on his own initiative and although Nash encouraged her team to think outside the box, that was with her knowledge and having been part of the discussion. Detectives going rogue she frowned upon and didn't encourage in any way, shape, or form, and that included her DSs. This was something Moretti couldn't let go. The train had left the station and he was happy to drive it alone.

As he walked the corridor towards the stairs, he paused. The more he considered what he'd done the more he thought it was a bad idea. He shrugged it off and pushed through the doors and bounded up the stairs two steps at a time until he was on the floor for the incident room. He paused on the small landing where he took a deep breath and entered.

Chapter Thirteen

Nash peered over the shoulder of DS Matthews as he opened the computer file from the port's authority in Northern Ireland. Matthews had not expected his request for information about frequent bike movements to be acknowledged so quickly. Mainly because the ferry was full of bikers who used the boat to travel between Northern Ireland and Scotland. Matthews had asked for the CCTV supervisors to look out for a Kawasaki motorcycle, dark in colour, with a passenger wearing a reflective jacket, that might have taken the ferry from Scotland to Ireland at some time between the dates of the two murders.

Nash had been keen that all bases were covered until they had official confirmation. She needed to know where this bike was travelling to and from, and whether there was a pattern of travel and times. Nash had also left messages for Boyle, but she'd experienced the same radio silence as Moretti.

'Do you think they've identified a possible bike?' Nash asked, while they waited for the video file to download.

Matthews leant his head back. 'It would appear they have,' he replied, pointing at a sentence above the video attachment that read "take a look at this".

Nash sat alongside Matthews. She checked her watch and wondered where Moretti was. She needed to speak with him, and no one had seen him since he left for a smoke. Finally, the video loaded, and they watched as a black Kawasaki Ninja 750cc appeared on the ANPR gate at the port, having just come off the ferry from Cairnryan, Scotland. It was leaving with one rider. The camera picked it up outside the port where another person got on the back. This person was dressed in a yellow sleeveless jacket. They'd been collected outside in a car park.

'It looks similar to the bike seen in Glasgow, wouldn't you say?' Matthews said. He pressed some keys and brought up the footage Police Scotland had provided of the bike that had been seen near the estate at the time of the shooting.

'The footage from the estate isn't great – very dark – so it's not easy to tell but the shape looks similar, and the passenger is wearing a similar style yellow vest,' Nash said.

Matthews had recorded the index number of the motorbike seen leaving the ferry terminal and ran it through the Police National Computer.

'We have a hit and it's a London address,' he said, pressing another button, and a printout of the registered keeper of the bike churned from the printer. Matthews collected it and handed a copy to Nash.

'Set a raid up, Owen,' she said, and went to find Moretti.

* * *

The motorbike was registered to a Gareth O'Connell and had been for over three years. From what the computer told Nash he'd been keeping it insured through a local insurance company in Eltham. As Nash studied the report, she rattled her pen in between her teeth.

She placed the printout down and stared out of her window. She wondered if she'd been too quick to act by raiding the address. Matthews knew that the operation would include an armed entry team, as the murder weapon may be with O'Connell. What if she strolled up and knocked on the door and just asked to speak with the registered keeper? What if she got a section of her team to sit up on the address and wait for O'Connell to leave on the bike and have him stopped and detained on the street? What if? The question that continually cropped up on a daily basis with no certainty of an answer. This was a murder investigation. There were two recent deaths. Both close in time and linked with her cold case.

No. She'd do things exactly as she'd tasked Matthews to arrange. It was better to be safe than sorry. She'd had enough surprises and didn't need any more.

Moretti rapped twice on Nash's open door and stepped across the threshold.

'Finally. Where have you been?' she asked.

Moretti was carrying two takeaway coffees from the cafe opposite the base. He handed Nash one, and he took the other and sat in an easy chair.

'Oh dear… a latte from outside and that look you get when you think you may have fucked up and ought, with hindsight, to have come to see me first. Am I right?' Nash said.

Moretti took a sip of his drink.

'Ye of little faith. I thought I'd bring you a drink. I was over the road getting a sandwich in the cafe,' he said, avoiding Nash's intense eyes. 'I see Owen is all over the armed entry for later,' Moretti added, a note of regret in his voice that he hadn't been given the job of putting that together.

Nash noted the tone.

'I would have had you arrange the fun but I couldn't find you,' she said. She set her large takeaway cup down on her desk. 'Do you think I've been hasty, Nick?'

'How do you mean?' he asked.

'With going to Northern Ireland and Scotland when we didn't need to,' she said, as she undid the scrunchy and let her hair cascade onto her shoulders. She grabbed her coffee and leant back in the office chair.

'Depends.'

'On what?' she asked.

'On whether we get a result or not,' Moretti said, flicking some fluff from his Paul Smith suit jacket.

Moretti watched his boss. He wondered if this was the time to tell her about McLachlan's call and his visit to the source unit, but dismissed it. He'd made his bed and would sleep in it.

'Right. I can't sit here drinking coffee all day. Grab a car, will you. Let's head over to Eltham and Owen can follow up. He can handle the briefing of the entry team, be good for his development,' she said.

Moretti was up and out the door before her. He patted his pockets for the car keys and went for his incident bag.

Chapter Fourteen

The briefing went well, and the firearms lead had decided she'd rather breach the address in the early hours of the morning. Nash had instructed Jonesy to keep watch on the house and ensure it was occupied when they entered. Nash needed someone inside if the gun was there. Jonesy was in an observation van that was left in an ideal location to observe the front door of the terraced property. He'd sent a text to say that he had observed O'Connell at the address. Research had shown that O'Connell was known to the police for various motoring offences as well as an assault on an officer for which he'd served six months' imprisonment. Jonesy had O'Connell's custody-imaging photo so he recognised him when he was putting his bin out for collection.

It was 5 p.m. by the time Nash and Moretti left the area to wait in Moretti's boat at the marina. Nash had instructed her team, who'd be involved in the search and security of O'Connell, to be back and ready to go at 1 a.m.

At Moretti's boat, Nash made the decision they should get a takeout before they went back to Eltham. The night was sure to be long and who knew how the arrest phase would play out. You could plan for every eventuality, but it was always the unknown that bit you in the arse and caused a simple job to become a lengthy one.

Nash sat and looked out of the window that overlooked the marina. The sun was setting and cast a deep red glow across the water. The light reflected from the hull of the boats and appeared to set them alight. Her phone rang. She hoped it was DC Boyle or DI Gordon returning her call, but she was to be disappointed.

'Nash,' she said, and waited for the caller to introduce themselves.

A quiet voice came on the line.

'Good evening, DI Nash, this is Greg Fielding from the National Crime Agency, is it a good time to talk?'

Nash didn't know anyone from the NCA and wondered how this Greg person had her number.

'Yes, how can I help you?' Nash put the call on speakerphone.

'I'm an intelligence officer with the NCA and I got your contact details from the Confidential Unit with the Met. Do you have a DS Nicholas Moretti working for you?' he asked, casually.

Nash looked at Moretti then took the phone off speaker. She remained in the room as she stared at Moretti who appeared genuinely confused at the question. It was a mystery to him as he hadn't called the NCA and had no live jobs running that could cross over with them.

'Yes, he's my DS. How can I help you?' she asked.

'He tasked your source unit with identifying a missing person from Scotland where he provided a call box number. That call box and the subject of the enquiry is, let's just say, of interest to me. We need to meet, DI Nash,' he said.

Nash watched the water lap against the hulls of the boats.

'How urgent is this? I have a live operation this evening,' she said.

'I know all about that armed operation. I would like to meet you tomorrow morning at eight, if possible, provided the operation tonight doesn't necessitate an NCA response,' he said.

Nash now directed her gaze at Moretti who sat sheepishly on his sofa, an empty beer in his sweaty grip.

'I have your number and will see you at your offices in Vauxhall at 8 a.m.,' Nash replied, then waited for Fielding to acknowledge and terminated the call.

She stood, hands on her hips, her eyes fixed on her DS. 'Out with it, Nick,' she said.

Moretti shuffled forward in his seat, his palms out in submission. Moretti explained the call from McLachlan and what he'd asked the Silverfox to do. Nash had chosen to sit for his explanation and was glad she had as she could feel the rage rise within her at her DS's umbrage to go behind her back on a tasking that should have come through her. If he'd told her, she could have thought through tactics rather than leaping on the first one. Moretti had lit a fuse she was unable to stamp out now it had exploded in the NCA. What was galling to her was that she'd been ambushed by this Greg Fielding and made to look incompetent as she hadn't a clue what Fielding was referring to.

Moretti finished his explanation and sat back.

'Is that all of it?' she asked.

'Yes,' he said.

'So, it's obvious to me that the NCA has an interest in Scotland. An interest that has been piqued thanks to you. Why didn't you tell me what had happened? Why didn't you tell me that McLachlan had called and that she'd been fearful enough to use a call box, so her personal phone data didn't appear on yours? Did that act not indicate that the shit could hit the fan or that it already had? Did you not stop to think why she'd contacted you, of all people, rather than anyone on her own force? Sometimes, Nick, I wonder if you're up to this type of work or whether you're burnt-out and need a new direction,' she said.

Moretti tried to rebut her, but she continued, 'I'm making an honest observation based on this incident and frankly your past behaviour on certain occasions has had me concerned. You're either out of your depth or not firing on all cylinders and need a change of scene.' She leant forwards resting her elbows on her thighs.

Moretti couldn't meet her gaze.

'So what are you saying? I should look for another post?' he said, mirroring her position at the edge of his seat. 'Because I'll quite happily go if that's what you want. Frankly, I think you're the one that needs a break. You returned too early after the stabbing and you've been at me ever since we went away. I can see it in your face even if you never voice it. The drinking, the gear in the boot of Boyle's car, and the odd look as I filmed while on the quad bike. It's called having fun, letting your hair down,' he said, exasperated, but he hadn't finished and was now on his feet pacing his own domain.

Nash remained where she was. She'd decided to let him run his mouth. She might learn something about him and what he was going through.

'I never complain, I just get on with the job and yes, when we went away, I partied a bit harder than I normally would, but what copper doesn't when they're away with the job – aside from you! I graft, ma'am. Yes, I get pissed but at least I'm not job pissed – I don't feel the same connection to work you do but I'll always act as best I can. That contact with the source unit was genuinely made to forward this investigation. Once I had something worthwhile to bring to you, I would have, but hey – shit happens and plans backfire,' he said. He grabbed his pipe and coat.

'I'll be outside. I need to calm down before I say something I regret. Give me five minutes and you're welcome to come up on the roof of the boat. If not, then you know where everything is. Help yourself.' With that, Moretti left Nash where she was and quietly closed the door to the boat as he exited.

Nash chewed the inside of her lip. His shot was clean and hit its mark, but she didn't take things personally. Years of fighting a male dominated system had hardened her. She had a soft side when it was required, but now wasn't the time. She decided to let Moretti have his space. She got her jacket and phone. As she opened the door to the boat, the pizza driver arrived, and Moretti was busy paying as Nash walked past.

'I'll be back at midnight,' she said as she strode out towards the car park where Moretti had left the work car.

She had more important issues to address. Her main concern was to learn as much as she could from the source handler before she met with Fielding in the morning. She had no intention of putting her officers or those of the armed entry team at further risk than they were. If there was pertinent information that was being withheld, she'd do her best to establish what that was. She suspected the covert network would prevent her by closing rank.

She phoned DS Dillon and arranged to meet the handlers in a neutral location. They were out and about and preferred not to return to the office. They arranged to meet centrally so Nash didn't have to travel far should Jonesy call her urgently from the observation van. She parked her car near Battersea power station and turned off the engine. It wasn't too long before a set of headlights swept her rear-view mirror and a car drew up alongside her. The window came down and the familiar faces of the source unit greeted her.

'Evening, Pip, sorry to have to meet like this. I had hoped Moretti would have at least informed you he'd spoken to us,' DS Dillon said.

The Silverfox was busy on a call, his mobile phone in his cupped hand. Nash beckoned Dillon out and he left his car and got into Nash's.

'What's going on? I've had a call from a Greg Fielding on the NCA and it would appear that Moretti's conversation with your DC has been fed back to them. I'm in the dark here and need you to shine some light. I have an armed operation in two hours as well as a meet with the NCA at eight,' she said.

Dillon leant into the passenger door as he spoke.

'Look, Pip, Nick came to us and said he'd taken a call from a PC in Glasgow who had a community contact who's now missing. He thought it was because of the murder up there. Moretti didn't give my handler much to go on other than the number the call was made from.' He paused, while he evaluated how much shit he was about to land Moretti in. 'That call box was, or still is, being monitored. Calls have been coming into the NCA from that box concerning an international drugs ring, cannabis mainly, but huge, and I mean huge amounts of the stuff that's getting through to other parts of Europe very easily. The NCA is of the view there's a conspiracy somewhere within the ports system that is facilitating the weed getting through. They were close until the male who was talking to PC McLachlan went missing. Now the intelligence feed's dried up. They wouldn't give me the name of the subject who was doing the talking, and the PC has done the right thing too by not saying who it was. DI Gordon knows, though. He was supposed to go and meet this fella and find out a name of the suspect for the murder but that never happened, as you know. The guy had a mobile he only ever used for scoring his smokes, but my money's on him being a runner and now he's dead. I wouldn't put it past the criminal organisation to have a tap on the phone too. Illegal, obviously. The NCA were going to get a sweep of the box to see. That's all I know. Frankly, I wish my handler never had agreed to help. My own DI is livid as he had the same call as you and he's not a happy man,' he said, wiping his cheeks with his palms.

Nash sat back. 'Thank you. Your handler didn't do anything wrong. My DS asked you and he did what was requested. If I'm being honest, it's a breakthrough – but don't tell Moretti that... not yet anyway,' she said, with a smirk reciprocated by Dillon.

'You have my complete confidence, ma'am,' he said, stifling a laugh.

He left and returned to his own car and departed the area. Nash gave them five minutes. Once they'd left, her phone rang – the name "Carl Harris" appeared on the screen and she answered it.

Chapter Fifteen

A frost gripped the pavements as the dead of night ticked over to a new day. Nash had collected Moretti who'd remained civil but subdued. She had driven them to the rendezvous point prior to the deployment. Jonesy had done his job well; he'd stayed awake, and O'Connell was still inside the house. Nash checked her watch – it was five minutes until show time. They'd chosen a car park to a main superstore for the RVP and Nash wondered just how many dealers and gun keepers were getting calls right now as her team were spotted arriving. Armed officers stepped out to get a leg stretch, and Nash did the same.

Nash caught the attention of the inspector in charge of the deployment who reminded her of a real-life Lara Croft. The inspector appeared as though she was going to war. She carried a Heckler and Koch MP5 across her chest and a 9 mm Glock strapped to her thigh. A patch depicting a silvery blue Union Jack with a thin blue line running through the middle sat above her name badge.

'Are we good?' the inspector asked Nash.

'We're good if you are. No change at the address according to my DC and no other update from me,' Nash said.

The inspector nodded her approval and checked her watch. Three minutes.

'Let's get this done then. Stay behind our van please, and do not deploy from your vehicle until I tell you it's safe to do so. Remain well away from the target address and please don't impede the arrival of the ambulance should we require it. I have to say this as you'd be surprised at just how cavalier some officers can be and blocking the only route in and out with a plethora of job cars isn't conducive to my team's safety,' she said, her face stoic and firm. There was to be no misunderstanding with this officer, and Nash respected that.

Nash got back into the car and Moretti started the engine having heard the conversation through the open window.

'Let's go then,' he said.

The car moved towards the now mobile armed response team van that motored with purpose across the empty car park and hit the main road towards the target address.

The convoy maintained the original order as they turned into the street where O'Connell lived. A full moon suspended above the roofs of the houses illuminated the street as the entourage trundled down the road, lights off. Moretti slowed and parked in the first available spot away from the main units. He turned off the ignition as the van approached the target address. With their engine off, and Moretti's window down, it became apparent that the van the armed officers were in had taken the same action. As it neared O'Connell's address, the van doors began to open, then the vehicle stopped.

Dark figures spilled out from the van, taking up various strategic positions across the street and around the house. Nash could feel her heart pound with anticipation. The door to O'Connell's house was whipped off its hinges. A cacophony of shouts of, 'Armed police, stay down, stay down,' could be heard, shattering the serenity of the street. Lights began to flick on at various houses.

Nash heard a thump on the roof of their car as though a cat had dropped onto it. She stepped out and looked on the roof. Nothing. Her attention was drawn to a sock on the ground near her door. From the strong smell she knew without looking it contained cannabis. Some bright spark had lobbed it from an upstairs window thinking they were the ones being raided. Which house or window was anyone's guess, as all the upstairs lights were out.

Nash's phone rang. It was the inspector from the firearms team.

'You can come up. All secure,' she said, and hung up.

'Let's go and see what we can find,' Nash said to Moretti.

O'Connell was sat, handcuffed, in a kitchen chair and visibly shaken. He'd offered no resistance and had been compliant when he'd been awoken by the armed team breaching his bedroom and ordering him to remain where he was and to keep his hands where they could be seen. One officer had found a blanket and had draped it around O'Connell's shoulders.

'L– look, I did my time for thumping one of you lot and I… I wasn't proud of what I done, but this takes the piss!' he claimed.

Nash moved forwards. 'I'm DI Nash. I have a warrant to search these premises,' she said, dropping a copy of the warrant in his lap.

'Is there anything here you shouldn't have, Mr O'Connell? It would save a lot of time and keep your house tidier if you tell me before I have my team start searching,' she said.

O'Connell's head remained low as his eyes read the warrant.

'I've no drugs here,' he said.

Nash let out a low sigh.

'Very well. We'll get on with what we came to do,' she said.

She turned and walked out towards the splinters of wood that were once a front door. She nodded to her search team who were all kitted up in forensic suits ready to begin. Moretti too. He was the team leader for this part of the operation. Nash stepped outside, and they all stepped in.

Chapter Sixteen

The search hadn't produced a gun or any ammunition. Nash's search team did discover documents that related to a Kawasaki motorbike and a bag of cannabis of a weight more than considered appropriate for personal use. They returned to Colindale police station where O'Connell was left in custody to get some sleep. In the meantime, Nash and Moretti had walked across the road to the office where they crashed in chairs for the night and grabbed what sleep they could before getting up and returning to Vauxhall for their meeting with Greg Fielding.

* * *

Nash and Moretti awaited collection by Greg Fielding in the reception area of the NCA building. Tired from a lack of sleep, the day stretched out before them after such an early start. The sullen security guard looked up from his paper and announced that Fielding would be with them presently. Presently was a further ten minutes. Moretti wished he'd used the time for a smoke rather than being contained in the stuffy environment called a reception area with little to no entertainment. It was as inviting as a holding area in a custody suite.

Finally, Fielding arrived. He was dressed in a herringbone jacket and trousers with a pair of brown brogues to finish off his hipster look. Moretti clocked the waistcoat beneath the jacket. A floral-patterned pocket square nosed out of the breast pocket. Fielding's blonde hair was tied off at the back in a short ponytail. Not Moretti's idea of style but he admired the man for not conforming to the habitual wear of an ex-police officer, which Fielding happened to be.

'Sorry for my late arrival. Some information received overnight had to be acted upon this morning. I'm all yours now. Do come this way,' he said with a public-school twang to his calm voice as he lead them out through the security doors of the reception into an outside area surrounded by office blocks.

The maintained grass area with planted borders served as a space for staff to relax in. They headed for some buildings nestled within the residential landscape beyond the security gates. Once they arrived at the correct building, Fielding swiped a card through a door lock entry system. They climbed a flight of stairs, arriving at a small room that looked like a storage area for exhibits but wasn't. Beyond the room was a set of double doors that Nash presumed led to the main office.

'Place all phones in these cages, please,' he said.

Fielding placed his phone in a small cage and closed and locked the door, removing the key and placing it in his waistcoat pocket. Nash and Moretti did the same and retained their own keys. It was protocol when entering a designated secure zone. Fielding took them through to a small meeting room off the open plan office and closed the door behind them as Nash and Moretti took a seat at the conference table.

'Anyone for coffee?' Fielding offered as he poured his own from a glass decanter.

Nash and Moretti nodded. They were both suffering from fatigue as they struggled to keep their eyes open after such a long day and night. They still had O'Connell to interview. Fielding brought the drinks over and began.

'So, I hear you have a man in custody from last night but no weapon?' he said.

'You're very well informed,' Nash said. No point asking how Fielding knew, he wasn't likely to say.

'Look, I appreciate you may feel hijacked around your investigation, but I assure you I'm here to help, not hinder,' Fielding said, flashing a quick smile.

'That's wonderful, Mr Fielding—'

'Please, call me Greg. I'm of equivalent rank to you,' he said, as he motioned with his hand that Nash should continue.

'Well, Greg, as I was saying – that all sounds wonderful but unless you have the gun and a suspect for the murder of Scott Whittaker, I fail to see how we can be of assistance to each other,' she said, returning his smile.

Nash threw it out there to see just how much Fielding would divulge. Sometimes people from different organisations couldn't stop themselves trying to be of use if they were desperate to jump on-board the others' investigation to save them time and effort with their own. Nash was prepared to find out.

Fielding leant down and brought up a battered leather briefcase. He opened it and produced a buff manila folder with a confidential marker on the top. He handed it to Nash.

'I've been informed you both have the appropriate management vetting to see this,' he said.

Nash took the file and opened it. Staring back at her was a picture of a Vietnamese male taken by a surveillance photographer. The male was wearing a dark business suit and shades and was in conversation with another man whose back was to the camera. This male with his back to the lens was wearing a tan overcoat and a woollen beanie hat pulled down to cover his hair. Other documents were attached: phone billing and NCA intelligence research.

'Very interesting, but what am I looking at?' Nash asked.

She knew Fielding had tried to play her by handing the docket over blind. She felt it was a tactic to assess her reaction. Fielding leant over and tapped the image with his pen.

'That man in the business suit is Quan Thao. He's a people trafficker. A supplier of human beings to work as horticulturists within the cannabis industry – grow house slaves,' Fielding said, leaning back.

'So where do we fit in? I'm concerned with the murder of Scott Whittaker and the recovery of a gun that's resurfaced after three years. I'm not having anything to do with drugs or people trafficking. You should talk to DC Boyle in Omagh he may be of more use than us,' Nash said as she closed the docket.

Fielding steepled his fingers.

'That's where you're wrong, Pippa, if I may be so formal. You see, if it wasn't for DS Moretti's association with PC McLachlan in Scotland, we wouldn't have had the breakthrough as early as we have,' he said.

Moretti shifted forwards ready to defend himself, but Nash held a hand across his chest, and he sat back.

'Get to the point, Greg. I have no time for games and neither does my DS,' she said.

'Very well. I'll explain what I can at this stage,' Fielding said and got up.

'DI Gordon has been assisting with the supply of information in relation to a major drugs ring that operates in Glasgow. I've tried to get a handover of the source of the information, but Gordon refuses to cooperate. His source, not ours. The information he shared was corroborated by other, let's say, more sensitive operational work of ours. But you can't beat ears on the ground.' He paused.

'We managed to ascertain who the source is by other means. Obviously, I can't tell you the identity of the person. We now need to speak with this individual as a matter of priority. Lives are at risk. PC McLachlan isn't aware of where the information is being disseminated. DI Gordon controls that. We know that she knows it must be critical to someone within the policing world, as DI Gordon insisted she tells him everything so a sterile corridor can be established between agencies. It helps her and prevents manipulation by the source. Her source is, or was, the eyes, ears and go-between for Quan Thao whom you've seen in the photo and the unidentified male he is seen speaking with. We believe the other man in the trench coat is his main intermediary in the UK for the export and importation of cannabis. Tonnes of the stuff. We aren't certain, but that's where we're at. When we searched the call box that PC McLachlan used to contact her source, it became clear she was getting involved in something way out of her depth. Once she had used the same call box to call you, DS Moretti, we had no option but to include you both. This criminal network is growing. They're not averse to clearing out anyone who may get in their way. Millions of pounds are at stake here and PC McLachlan, we believe, hasn't a clue what she's been drawn into by having contact with this source,' Fielding said, looking between Nash and Moretti.

Nash was thankful for Fielding's honesty. McLachlan had been used by both the male who was giving her information and her own DI. A man who, Nash thought, appeared to be using her to accelerate his career path. DI Gordon had been wise to advise McLachlan to use a call box. This way he could ensure that he was in control of any information gained. He was then able to choose what he wanted to share with Fielding. Nash was confident they'd seen who they assumed was the source in question, the guy smoking a joint outside the parade of shops close to the police office PC McLachlan used – and now he was missing.

'So how do we fit in? My investigation is London based. Once I have the reports back from the pathologist in Northern Ireland and Scotland as well as the bullets from both, so we can do our own forensic work, that will be me until I have the suspect and the gun,' Nash said.

Fielding looked to the ceiling before replying.

'I'm afraid you'll be waiting a long time for any of that,' Fielding said, a look of informed contempt across his tanned cheeks.

'I'm not following,' Nash said.

'There is no evidence in its physical form,' Fielding said.

'That's impossible. I've seen the ballistic reports from both Scotland and Northern Ireland. I saw photos of the bodies of each victim, and I've been to each scene,' Nash said.

Fielding walked to a one-way glass window that overlooked the main office, his hands stuffed in his pockets as he turned.

'The bodies never arrived at the coroner's office and the bullets are nowhere to be found,' Fielding said, with a note of despair in his voice.

Nash looked at Moretti.

'Bodies don't go missing from crime scenes, Greg. They were photographed in situ and collected by known firms called upon to do such a thing. When we were at the police station in Northern Ireland, we were informed that the exhibits had been removed to a central store. We were shown the empty exhibits room. I've been trying to get hold of both detectives ever since to ascertain where they are…' Nash's voice trailed off.

'We're not saying DI Gordon or DC Boyle *are* involved – yet. But that's only because we haven't got the evidence. I know you've seen the murder scene reports. I've instructed others within my network to speak with trusted people in Northern Ireland and Scotland. No one is saying that your Beretta pistol wasn't the weapon used or that the two murders never happened. Do you see why you needed to know, DI Nash? The more you were getting involved in enquiries that, to be frank, had no need for your intervention, the harder it was to keep the lid on everything – for us and them,' Fielding said.

Nash collapsed back in her seat and rest her hands atop her head.

'Another fine mess,' she said.

Fielding and Moretti both nodded. Nash wasn't finished.

'While I appreciate all you've told me, Greg, I don't appreciate being told where I can go in a murder investigation that's most definitely linked to mine here in London. I just need to shake the box and find the rogue pieces of the puzzle,' she said.

Fielding was far from done too.

'I would strongly advise, Detective Inspector, that you leave the puzzle and move onto a good book,' he said, with a fixed glare on Nash.

Chapter Seventeen

Nash and Moretti left Fielding and returned to Colindale to interview O'Connell. Neither of them had spoken during the tube journey, using the time to take in the new information. No wonder the NCA were involved, Nash thought. This went way beyond an organised criminal network involved in people trafficking and cannabis farming. She knew they hadn't been told everything. The victims' bodies were missing and Fielding, by all accounts, hadn't a clue where or how that had happened, or wasn't saying. Surely someone would have spoken with the people tasked with the removal of the bodies to the mortuary in anticipation of the post-mortem.

If they'd been spoken to, why hadn't Fielding told her? It was an obvious question that Fielding must have known would occur to her. She hadn't voiced her concerns as he had made it clear that he wasn't there to answer questions.

He was there to give her a warning. She and Moretti were treading on toes by pursuing this matter.

To Fielding, this wasn't about charging the right person or providing closure for Whittaker's family. This was about organised crime and corruption. Nash knew from her UCO work that drugs didn't simply arrive in the UK by the tonne. There had to be connections at either end to enable the drugs to move undetected and that meant paying the right people, in the right positions, good money to ensure it reached its intended destination.

She'd spoken to Moretti on the walk to Vauxhall tube station about the low-level threat to his life Fielding had inferred but hadn't backed up with anything concrete. Moretti had shrugged it off. How could his brief association with PC McLachlan and one phone call place him at immediate risk of harm? There'd be time to discuss it all once they'd spoken with O'Connell. Fielding hadn't said they shouldn't interview him, he'd simply asked to be informed of the result. Nash had assured him she'd let him know exactly what was said.

* * *

The interview room felt cold and there was nothing that could be done to warm it up. It would have to do, Nash thought. She adjusted her chair opposite O'Connell who sat waiting for the recorded interview to begin. Nash had conducted the legal preamble and once she was satisfied, she nodded at Moretti and cracked on.

'Mr O'Connell, as you are aware, you're in custody as a result of a warrant executed at your premises in the early hours of this morning where a substantial package of cannabis was found.'

'That's right,' O'Connell replied.

'I don't wish to question you further about that as you admitted it was yours last night and signed an officer's notebook to this effect. What I'm interested in is documents in relation to a Kawasaki Ninja motorcycle found at your premises, a V5 registration document in fact.'

Nash waited. O'Connell stared back at her bemused at how easy this appeared to be.

'Yes, that was at my house. I don't think that's a criminal offence, Inspector,' he replied, with a genuine look of bewilderment upon his face.

'Mr O'Connell, can you explain where you've been with the bike over the last month?' Nash said.

She sat back, giving O'Connell the space to reply. O'Connell rubbed the stubble on his chin and wiped his hand through his thinning brown hair.

'I can tell you exactly where it's been. At Motorcycle City garages. It was in for a respray and engine overhaul,' he said.

Nash squinted as though the overhead strip light had suddenly taken on a new lease of life.

'I see, and the garage would corroborate this?' Nash questioned.

'I bloody hope so, but now you're here with me you might be able to explain something that's confused me in the last week,' O'Connell said.

Nash nodded for him to continue.

'Well, I took the bike in two weeks ago and I wondered if your robust actions were in relation to an unpaid speeding fine,' he said.

Nash looked confused at where O'Connell was going.

'I don't understand, Mr O'Connell. We don't deploy armed teams for outstanding fines collection. Perhaps you could enlighten us,' she said.

O'Connell laughed.

'I was hoping you would be the ones who could enlighten me, Inspector, as I don't know how my bike could have been in two places at once, especially with an engine that's so poor. It was a miracle it ticked over let alone activated a speed camera,' he said, chuckling to himself.

Nash glanced at Moretti who shrugged.

'Where was this offence meant to have taken place?' Nash asked.

'Glasgow of all places! I've never been to Scotland in my life let alone taken my bike there. The puzzling thing for me was that an image on the ticket clearly showed my registration number. Shame it wasn't my bike,' he said, shaking his head at the situation he'd found himself in.

'Where is this ticket now?' Nash asked.

'In my wallet with the big lump of a man behind the desk,' O'Connell said, in reference to the custody sergeant.

'Best I take a look at that ticket, Mr O'Connell,' Nash said. She recited the time, suspended the interview, and switched off the recorder.

With O'Connell safely back in his cell, Nash obtained the personal property taken from O'Connell on arrival at the station. There, in his wallet, was the ticket issued in Glasgow as he'd described.

'Someone's cloned his plates,' Nash said.

Moretti continued to riffle through the other contents of the wallet. He pulled out a leaflet on multiple sclerosis.

'I imagine this is why he had all that weed on him too. I have a friend who uses it for pain, and he swears by it. Way better than any prescribed drug and not as addictive,' he said.

Nash leant on the raised desk that separated the custody sergeant from the prisoners. She pushed the property back into a new clear exhibits bag, resealed, and signed it.

'I'll make the arrangements with the prisoner processing unit to caution him for possession of cannabis,' Nash said.

Moretti nodded and waited for a custody sergeant to become free. Nash left the custody suite to send Jonesy to the garage to make sure someone had eyes on the bike, but she was satisfied with the account given by O'Connell.

Chapter Eighteen

Nash dispensed with the formality of the briefing room and went straight to the incident room to bring her team up to speed with O'Connell's interview. Jonesy confirmed the garage had the bike. He'd videoed the frame and index number and sent it to Nash.

'Right, I appreciate all the hard work you're doing on the Whittaker case. I also appreciate that some of you may feel you've not progressed the Whittaker murder while I've been off to Scotland and Northern Ireland on enquiries over there. What I can say is you'd be wrong in that assumption.'

She paused and assessed the eyes of those she knew would have been thinking exactly that.

'O'Connell's motorbike would appear to have been cloned. A motorbike with his registration was caught in a mobile speed trap in Glasgow on the day of the murder. DS Matthews has the image and is getting the original shot enhanced. There were two on the bike. The rear passenger dressed in a yellow vest top over his coat. This same bike is believed to be one leaving the ferry terminal at Northern Ireland a day after the murder. So where does that leave us?'

Nash adjusted her seated position. Her team remained impassive. Some sat up right, others slouched and rubbed their eyes. Nash was faced with a unique situation since she couldn't divulge the NCA involvement. She didn't want many ears with the knowledge either. Should there be any leak, the NCA would be hammering down the Met's door first before they looked closer to home. She wouldn't accept that here and with her staff.

'I've discussed a number of actions with DS Moretti who will talk with George afterwards…' Nash said.

'Why can't you tell me direct? I hate getting actions third hand and we all know Moretti's brain's fried,' Sagona said, drumming his sausage-like fingers against the ridge of his gut.

Moretti ignored the barb as he concentrated on Nash. This was all new to him. Nash continued.

'It will be Nick, because as of now I'm on leave. I've been granted a week's annual and I've accepted it. Nick will be acting DI while I'm gone.'

The room dropped in volume after the initial mutterings of discontent. It wasn't unreasonable to expect that the Investigating Officer who'd resurrected a cold case would hang around to see it through the initial fortnight, even more so when two other murders were linked via forensics. Moretti scratched his head, and Nash brought the meeting to a close.

'With that, I'll have a quick word with Nick, and see you in a week,' Nash said.

She stood up and pushed her skirt straight. Moretti followed her out, walking backwards and shrugging at the team before he turned through the door after Nash.

'Close the door please,' Nash said.

Moretti did as she asked and sat opposite her at her desk.

'I apologise for bombarding you in there, but I've literally made the decision now. I'll get the nod from the DCI if I can get him away from whatever lunch he's on in the city. You were right, Nick. I need a break. All's in hand here and you can adequately hold the fort for a week while I'm away. My leg's been throbbing around the impact site where the blade went in, and along with your reminder, it seems pertinent I get away,' she said.

Moretti leant back and let out a sigh.

'I can't say I'm glad you listened, Pip. I haven't the foggiest where to go with this right now. The NCA and

Fielding have thrown a huge spanner in the works. What can I tell that lot out there? You'll have to tell me something to say as I haven't a Scooby,' Moretti said, getting up. He leant against the window ledge.

Nash closed her eyes for a beat.

'Nick, just keep things going here on what we have. Make sure the index number is all over ANPR and also contact traffic command and brief them so all their shifts know too. At least we can cover pan-London with them. If the bike turns up in an accident, it will be flagged on PNC, so hopefully the first responder will be aware there are firearms associated with the bike. They can, hopefully, keep it clean forensically with the rider and bike if they're with it. As for the Beretta, get on to the source unit and get them working it up again with their sources. The enhanced reward has been authorised. It's ten grand for any information that leads to the recovery of the gun and the arrest and charge of the suspect. That might get some tongues wagging. Otherwise, take this time to get to know what it's like to be sat where I am. Use my office but don't leave crumbs on the desk, and please water the plant,' Nash said.

She got up and grabbed her coat and bag. Her eyes scanned the room for anything else she'd need as her work phone pinged. She glanced at the screen, a message from DS Carl Harris. A simple thumbs up emoji.

'Are you staying at home if I need to get hold of you?' Moretti asked, turning back from the window.

'I'll be out of contact. Next person is the DCI for anything you require. Good luck and thank you, Nick,' she said, patting him on the shoulder as she walked out of her office.

Moretti remained where he was. He looked at the chair she'd just occupied. A chair he wondered if he was fit to fill. He was soon to find out. Nash's desk phone rang and Moretti picked it up.

'DI Moretti, how can I help?' he said, pulling a paper and pen towards him.

Chapter Nineteen

'Thank you,' Nash said, accepting the gin and tonic from the air steward. Nash dropped the seat tray and set her drink down. *Far from the Madding Crowd* by Thomas Hardy, her choice of entertainment for the flight.

As she settled in with her cloth-bound edition of the book, she recalled a time she'd lent Moretti *On Chesil Beach*. He'd asked her what she was reading when he'd caught her having a five-minute lunch break in the office. His summation of the entire novel was reduced to how he hadn't cared if the narrator got his leg over on his wedding night and had given up halfway. That was all Nash needed to know about Moretti's appreciation of literature. An announcement came over the tannoy informing the passengers that the aircraft would shortly be making its descent. Nash clicked the seat belt into place and put her book in her bag under the seat.

The aircraft breached the clouds, and the patchwork quilt of fields revealed themselves below. She closed her eyes and breathed evenly as the plane approached the landing strip. She felt the thump of the wheels beneath her locking into position, and then the plane touched down on the runway. The wing flaps flipped, and the brakes screamed. There was a roar of wind then the plane slowed to a crawl. Soon enough the sign to unclip seat belts pinged overhead, and like Pavlovian dogs the passengers jumped up as one and began releasing the overhead lockers in desperation to be reunited with their luggage.

Nash remained as relaxed as a lioness after a good hunt. No point in rushing.

Nash was through the gates into the arrivals terminal in no time. She'd only packed what could be carried and stored in an overhead locker. She'd purchase any other clothing she might need while she was at her rented place. As she exited the arrivals, she felt the sense of familiarity that comes when you visit the same destination every holiday. The sun was low and affected her vision, but the transport she'd booked was parked across the road from where she stood. The outline of the conveyance familiar, as was the sun-framed silhouette of her driver who now began to walk towards her. She pulled her shades from her jacket pocket and put them on. The silhouette took the form of exactly the person she wished to see. Will Boyle took off his hat as though he was greeting royalty, and with a dip of his head, he addressed Nash.

'Now then, Pip, you're back earlier than I expected, so you are. Always good to see the cottage used, especially when I know the person who'll be using it… unlike the last tenant,' he said, raising his eyes as he took hold of her case.

Nash smiled. 'Good to be back, Will, and thanks for letting me use it at short notice. I needed a break. The last time was too quick. All work no play,' she said.

She opened the door to the truck and got in. There was no trailer of livestock this time, and Nash relaxed in the twin seats as she leant against the door and waited for Will to join her.

'So, will you be needing to stop anywhere before we start, or can I motor home? I have the sheep to get in and by the looks of the clouds this is the last we'll be seeing of the dry. I can't stand herding them when it's dark and wet,' Will announced, his eyes returning from the sky back to Nash.

'Home, James,' Nash said.

Will started the engine, and they set off. The going was good, and Will soon relaxed into the drive. He was a keen talker and Nash let him have the floor. He explained how his brother had also taken a few days' leave, but when Will had told him she was coming, he'd said he'd try to see her before she left. Nash shrugged off any notion of seeing DC Pete Boyle. That wasn't her priority.

Will whiled away the journey with tales of rural life. She learnt a lot about Will now that she was here as a guest. Will had been open with her, explaining how he was coping with the farm on his own. His wife had left him taking the two children. Community bonds were strong, and Nash wondered where she'd gone but refrained from asking too many questions.

She could have chosen anywhere in the world to take a holiday, and only she knew why she'd chosen to return to the cottage in a valley tainted by death. She thought about what Moretti had said about her being job pissed. Obsessed with duty was the polite way he could have put it, but that wouldn't have conveyed the message as strongly. Not with her. It was a message designed to hit home. She wasn't cut from the same blue serge as many of her rank and service. She was proud and protective of that. Nash knew her mind and was confident to act on it when needed.

She felt guilt at leaving Moretti at short notice, but she'd done it with the best of intentions. The sun had now dipped beyond the mountains and an amber haze hung above the horizon as they got closer to Will's farm. Nash had been so deep in thought she hadn't noticed they'd arrived at the foot of the track that led to the farm and were now on the approach to the gate. Will slowed the truck and stopped. He let the engine run.

'I'll be getting the gate, you wait there,' he said.

The familiar clang of metal and the yap of his Jack Russell greeted him.

Will drove Nash to the cottage. The rain had been scarce, and the ground was dry so there was no need to use the quad bikes. Nash grabbed the interior handle with both hands and gripped as she was thrown about.

'I'll be a bruised wreck by the time we get there,' she joked.

Will eased off the accelerator and nodded with his chin in apology. He parked up and jumped out of the truck to get her case.

'I had the fire going and the heating on before I came for you,' he said, opening the door and letting Nash step inside. 'I must leave you now. You know where I am should you need anything. I stocked up with the food you asked for too, so all that's left is to relax and enjoy your stay.'

With that, Will left and closed the door behind him.

Nash noticed the yellow vest Moretti had been wearing when she'd found him that morning, and she smiled at the sight as she took her case into the bedroom and placed it on a newly laundered bed.

'I hope I'm doing the right thing,' she said to the void and began to unpack.

Chapter Twenty

Moretti pinched the bridge of his nose and put the receiver down. He felt like smashing the phone due to the volume of calls that had been coming through since Nash left. He was still at the office despite the hour, as were a few diehards who were either genuinely working or avoiding home and domestic disharmony. Moretti looked at the daybook pages he'd filled with his scrawl: requests for stats, demanding sets of figures for overtime, officers who hadn't completed their annual Officer Safety Training and a stationery cupboard review sent by JJ. He realised how much Nash had been fielding. He'd only been in her chair a day, and he felt as though he'd had no time to do any police work. The only responsibility Nash had delegated to him was that of vehicle fleet manager, and he'd delegated that to Jonesy before the ink had dried on Nash's memo.

There was a knock at the door and Matthews entered carrying a sheet of paper.

'Not that old trick,' Moretti said, nodding at the paper in Matthews's hand.

'Oh – this? No this is actual work, not a prop that purports to make me look as though I'm busy when I'm not,' Matthews said. He drew up a seat opposite Moretti and handed him the sheet.

'What is it?' Moretti asked in a civil way. He leant back in his chair in the same way Nash did when she looked at a fresh document for the first time.

'It's a printout of the index number of the motorbike. I took a liberty…'

Moretti raised his eyes. 'I hope it was legal?'

Matthews laughed.

'Absolutely. Look, I've a mate who has access to a system that crunches numbers. He works on the intelligence side of things for traffic and serious crime,' Matthews said.

'Traffic and serious crime alongside one another? What have we become?'

Moretti set the paper down and concentrated on what Matthews had to say now he'd seen the document, as it appeared to be a series of times, dates, numbers, and letters.

Matthews continued.

'I asked for the index of the bike to be run through his system. It's produced an amazing result for us. The bike is always in company with this car.'

He produced another PNC printout of a Volvo XC90, which was registered in London at a business address in the East End.

Moretti pushed the sheet back to Matthews.

'OK, so what do you recommend next? Visit the address?' Moretti asked.

Matthews sat and shook his head.

'No. I sent JJ to have a look, and he's seen the car at the venue. It's a warehouse that specialises in Vietnamese food for the restaurant trade. He lives a couple of miles from it. He was happy to make it part of his route home. I think we should do some digging and see who owns it. Take a look at the business's finances too,' Matthews said.

Moretti pondered the information. He was in a difficult position. He'd seen the NCA imagery of Quan Thao – and Matthews hadn't. Matthews was unaware of the NCA involvement and before Nash had left, she'd been adamant Moretti kept things tight. Stick with what they knew. He couldn't call her to ask advice as she was uncontactable. Moretti was the one in the chair, and Matthews knew it too. It was up to Moretti to make the choice. Moretti rocked from side to side in the office chair.

'Here's what I think. We get both index numbers flagged on the PNC and ANPR systems. Inform all ferry ports too via your own intelligence channels. I need to know how often these vehicles are together and where they go. No surveillance. Nash told me to hold the fort while she was away and to keep things tight. What else does the analysis show us?' Moretti asked.

'It shows that what you're asking has already been done,' he said.

Moretti studied the page again, and in particular the dates and times. The convoy used the same ferry from Northern Ireland once a month, and Matthews had even been able to track where they went from using various traffic cameras that had picked up the vehicles as they travelled.

Moretti had worked investigations where a package on the move would be watched by an escort that was often armed. Moretti surmised that if they were trafficking drugs together this could be a possibility, but he had no evidence to corroborate his thoughts. Any attention on the Volvo, and the guy on the bike would react. Whether that meant drawing away the unwanted attention of a police patrol or protecting the drugs from another gang intent on robbing them.

Moretti thought about how this helped the Whittaker enquiry. Scott Whittaker had nothing to do with drugs and yet it would appear he'd become trapped in the network's spokes and ended up murdered. Why? This very question had been troubling Nash for years.

'Owen, this is great stuff, but we can't do any more for now. At least not until Nash returns,' Moretti said to an astonished Matthews.

'Are you saying we sit on it?' he enquired with a look of confusion bordering on disgust.

'No. I'm saying we leave the flags on the PNC,' Moretti replied.

Matthews leant across the desk again and pushed the paper back to Moretti.

'We can't do that, Nick.'

'Why?'

'Because the data is telling us they could move again. The gun that killed our victim could be on-board that motorbike and we have no idea where to look for it. It's not on the mainland though, as it's coming here on the ferry. As is the Volvo. That too has been documented leaving the same ferry as the bike. The bike then catches up with the Volvo once they're on the A75 in Scotland,' Matthews said.

Moretti swallowed. If he let it run, he risked losing the gun and a possible suspect. They could also kill again. They may change tactic and go to ground. They'd be back to square one. Moretti also knew if word got out that the actual owner of the bike had been arrested then they could switch transport. There was nothing to say the garage where O'Connell's bike lay in bits wasn't connected. Moretti wasn't questioning the garage owner's integrity, but it had to be acknowledged as a risk.

Moretti rubbed his eyes. He was happy taking decisions, but this was different. The implications were vast, and he had no intention of calling Fielding at the NCA or anyone like Boyle or Gordon. He leant forwards and looked at Matthews.

'Owen, you know what it's like to be sitting here. It's shit, and we both know that, but what if I fuck up by getting a team briefed and ready to take these two out and they're on a dummy run? Everything would be blown. The way Nash feels about my work performance would mean I'd be back in a borough CID office shovelling more shit than a farmer. I wouldn't put it past Pip to know this would all blow up, so she took flight and placed me here to test me and show me up,' he said.

Matthews stood up and leant on the desk between them, his eyes narrowed.

'That's bollocks and you know it. She'd *never* do that to any of us. She looked after me when professional standards were breathing down my neck and put her own head on the block. As did you. Take a decision, Nick. Any decision taken in good faith is better than not taking one at all,' Matthews said.

He walked over to the window and lifted the watering jug and dispensed a glug into the geranium.

'You're right, Owen. I'm sticking with my earlier choice. Have the PNC show that I'm to be contacted should either the bike or Volvo be spotted together. I'll reassess my options then,' he said.

'Yes, Guv,' Matthews replied, with a warm smile and a nod of his head.

* * *

Moretti took the work car home in case he needed to respond to any urgent call from the team. He sat in his chair nursing a Scotch, phone in hand. He scrolled through the photos on his phone and arrived at the video footage he'd taken on the quad bike at Will's farm. He played it and reminisced at how good the freedom had felt bombing around the pasture on a huge beast of a bike without a care in the world. He'd caught Pip too. Her hair billowed out above the collar of her jacket as she rode. The video continued to the arrival at the cottage, and he'd captured DC Boyle's car in the final frame. His brain was triggered as though a switch had flicked. He paused the video and drew his finger left across the footage bar and played it again.

Where the camera had caught Boyle's car, there was a yellow reflective vest draped across the back of the passenger seat. What struck Moretti about this was the outline of the neck of the garment. It looked familiar. Moretti stared at his drink. Just another hi-vis vest. The damn things were everywhere he looked.

He laughed at the memory of waking up in one when he'd been rolled down the hill drunk. Drunk. He looked at his glass and back at the bottle of Scotch. He had to change. He stared across at a small shelf near his LPs and his eyes came to rest on an ashtray next to his pipe. Within it was a dark object. He scooped it up and returned to his armchair and sat down.

Pulling the bottle of Scotch closer, he leant back and held up the memento he'd brought back from his trip, rolling the spent bullet in his fingertips. Moretti had dug the bullet out of the quarry stone after he'd finished shooting with Boyle. He laughed as he remembered the banter they'd had as they fired off round after round into the wooden targets Boyle had erected. They'd laughed about the job and how it sucked the joy out of life, but it made up for it when you had trips away with work.

He raised his feet onto the low coffee table in front of him and downed the whisky from his glass. He tipped the neck of the bottle and poured himself another good measure. Fuck it, he thought, you only live once.

Chapter Twenty-One

Nash had arisen early. As she opened the cottage door, she nearly tripped over a box of fresh eggs. Will had left them and attached a note with a contact number. He was taking sheep to market and wouldn't be back until late. She placed the eggs and note in the porch and closed the door.

She left the cottage unlocked and hid the key under a stone. A habit from her own parents' house but that was when she lived there, and they only had one key between the three of them. She set off down the narrow grass track that was formed by the feet of many sheep and left the path for others who'd follow them. The track skirted the edge of the entrance to the bunker. As she got close, she felt a shiver down her neck at the thought of the poor victim who'd suffered so much.

As she stopped and looked at the metal cap that was the entrance, she noticed something had changed. It was welded shut. There was a belt of weld wound around the circumference of the steel lid. Never to be entered or lifted again. They'd clearly no intention of going back down there and didn't want a repeat of what had happened.

She crouched down and pulled up a clump of grass. The soil remained attached as she ran the contents through her fingers. She thought about the previous conversations with Fielding and looked up at the ridge in the distance. She discarded the grass in her hand and began the climb to the summit of the mountain where she'd decided she'd run the ridgeline before lunch.

* * *

Moretti placed the paracetamol he'd discovered in Nash's drawer at the back of his tongue. He washed them down with black coffee. He'd slept poorly and used this to his advantage by setting off for work at 5 a.m. and beating the gridlock that London's roads soon became after six. His head was thumping. He poured himself a fresh coffee and sat in one of Nash's meet and greet seats.

He took out a couple of albums of scene photos from the Whittaker case. He leafed through the first album. Most of the shots showed the general scene from a distance, many taken at various angles. As the tablets began to kick in, he felt that he might have the stomach to look at the ones of Whittaker. He came to one of the recovery trucks and paused. What struck Moretti was that the absence of a vehicle on the back of it.

He hadn't been on the original enquiry and wondered why that would be. The next image showed Whittaker slumped against the door of the recovery truck's cab. To Moretti it appeared as though the position of the body was indicative of him trying to enter the cab of the truck when he was killed. Had Whittaker seen the gun and tried to escape by getting back in the lorry, or had he been about to leave and was shot from behind? Moretti recalled that Whittaker had been sent to the location to collect a vehicle, so where was it? He made a note in his daybook and closed it.

He heard snoring and left Nash's office. He entered the main incident room and found Matthews slumped in a chair. He was fast asleep, covered by a thin blue blanket used in the cells. His feet were propped on another chair. Moretti paused, returned to Nash's office, and poured another coffee before returning with his own.

'Wake up, Owen,' he said, wafting the mug under Matthews's nose.

Matthews stirred and his eyes flickered open.

'Jesus, what time is it?' he asked, accepting the drink from Moretti.

'Too early, my friend. Why are you here? I can tell by your clothes you haven't been home,' Moretti asked.

Matthews turned away from Moretti. He yawned and scratched his head. He sat up in his seat and Moretti could tell by the way Matthews's head drooped what was coming next.

'The wife kicked me out.'

Moretti's head drew back like a pigeon.

'You're the last person I'd expect to hear that from. Is there anything you need?' Moretti said.

Matthews stood up and stretched.

'Nah, I had it coming to be fair. Working all hours and never being at home meant she'd more time to explore a life without me – a new regime of fitness, and a personal trainer. He's been incredibly attentive to every aspect of her body,' he said as he suppressed a laugh.

Moretti felt terrible for him. Owen did nothing but work and adored his wife. If there was overtime going, he'd be there, and she'd always encouraged him to earn.

'I'll be going to my brother's place for a bit but last night he had a guest and wanted some space – so he asked if I could wait a night before I arrived and took over his spare room. Now you're here I have some other news I think you'll like. First off, I need to shower,' Matthews announced. He took a towel from under his desk and patted Moretti on the shoulder as he passed.

Moretti took the decision to get breakfast. He and Matthews left for a twenty-four-hour cafe a short drive away. As they waited for the food, Matthews regaled Moretti with what he'd managed to glean from his overnight enquiries.

'I used the time to go over the Whittaker case and look at any areas that needed more work or anything Nash's previous team had missed. It was thorough, I'll give her that, but there was one aspect that cropped up.' Matthews paused, stuffing a forkful of bacon in his mouth like he hadn't eaten in a week. 'I wanted to know more about Mrs Whittaker. There'd been a major focus on Scott, naturally – who he was and why he would be the target of a drive-by shooting. His wife had the usual background stuff and research package. But I felt there was no meat on the bones,' he said.

Moretti nodded as he ate, and Matthews placed his cutlery down as he continued. He glanced up at the ceiling as he organised his thoughts before speaking.

'I ran some additional checks on her, nothing out of the ordinary, what we've always done with any of our jobs, but I guess other teams aren't as robust. I say this because a search on the Crime Recording Information System, going back three years from now, showed that she'd reported getting nuisance calls that began two days after Scott was murdered.' Matthews stabbed at a sausage.

'Who reported it?' Moretti asked.

'She didn't mention a thing to her family liaison officer. She phoned it through and reported it separately. It was marked up for no further action as the calls were made from an unregistered mobile phone and the calls were all silent, so she said. Her billing was obtained and from the record on the CRIS system, it didn't correlate.'

'How come?' Moretti asked.

'The duration of the calls recorded on her phone data did not indicate that she'd hung up immediately as she claimed. She was either listening and asking who it was or there was a brief conversation, and she was telling them to stop,' Matthews said.

They both ceased talking as the cafe owner topped up their mugs from a coffee jug. When he'd left, Moretti spoke.

'Did anyone from the police speak with her about it?'

Matthews shook his head. 'From what I could see they marked it up as record only on the request of the victim. Someone must have considered it was worth getting her call data though, and she must have consented to that despite the apparent apathy to pursue things further. Very strange if you ask me.' He sipped his coffee.

Moretti leant back and rested his hands at the back of his head as he stared out of the cafe's window at the street.

It was strange. What was worse was that nobody had looked into any potential link with the murder of her husband. Moretti dropped his hand and leant closer towards Matthews.

'Was there any mention of the murder on the nuisance call report?' Moretti asked.

'Not that I could see. No one from Nash's shooting team was notified, why?'

'That caller could have been her husband's killer and for whatever reason she didn't think to mention it,' Moretti said, wiping his lips with a paper napkin and started to get up.

'We off already?' Matthews asked.

'Time we visited Whittaker's wife again – don't you think?' Moretti said.

Matthews nodded and grabbed the last slice of toast. Moretti left the cash on the table and they waved the cafe owner farewell.

Chapter Twenty-Two

Nash leant into the wind as she ran along the ridgeline. Below her she could see the granite walls of the quarry where Moretti and Boyle had played guns. The blistered targets still stood thanks to the semi-circle of stone that shielded the wooden structures from the wind.

The wind was now whipping across her face and she felt she couldn't remain at this height so she followed the path down the side of the mountain back to the floor of the quarry. She'd run a new route back to the cottage where she anticipated a relaxing bath and a decent fry-up. As she began her descent, she recognised a sensation arise in her that she hadn't felt until this point of her run. A sense she was being watched.

She realised how absurd this seemed as there was nothing to be seen and yet the feeling was there. She put the sensation down to her own observation of her vulnerability being so high without any support should she fall or anyone to call upon to help her. Her confidence began to return as she made her way towards firmer ground.

She wondered how Moretti was doing holding the fort without her. She hoped he was sticking to the script and not going off piste before she returned. Last thing she wanted was to walk back into a storm created by an overzealous DS. As soon as the negative voice appeared, she quashed it. She had faith in his abilities. She needed to show Moretti she did, despite the way she'd been with him over his drinking and general behaviour.

She hoped being put in charge would do him some good. Instil a level of responsibility beyond work, women, and drink. As she neared a copse of gorse the bush moved. She tried to stop, but her feet slipped. She hadn't anticipated the reaction and crashed to the ground. Her feet gave way under her as a mountain hare darted from the gorse and bounded off down the mountainside. Nash remained still. Her shin was grazed but not bleeding. Same for her elbows. She stared out over the valley floor that leaked away from her and she blinked away a tear. She knew why she'd returned to this place of beauty and death. Yet that knowledge wasn't enough.

She lay back and watched the cloud drift above her. She let her breathing regulate as she gathered her thoughts. How long would it take for the Whittaker case to be resolved, the gun and the bullets to be recovered and the file placed away never to be needed again? There'd be no room for any appeal once she finished with the investigation. She had every confidence in her team, and they didn't need her as much as they first had when she'd arrived as their new IO. They'd all grown in their ability to detect and bring to justice the worst offenders that haunted London. She'd done a good job there. She knew it. Her bosses knew it, and that was why she'd struggle to get her next rank if she stayed where she was.

She got up and dusted herself down of dirt and grass. She estimated she'd be back on the valley floor in an hour. She stretched her leg and arm muscles and set off. Gradually she got back into her stride down the mountainside. She began to feel the spring return to her step as her arms pumped. Her legs and body warmed with the confidence and energy that only came with hard work and overcoming adversity.

Dark cloud drifted above her as she slowed to a walk. Her feet welcomed the level ground of the quarry floor. She gave a clap as she stared at the stone walls interspersed with pools of water and ferns. The echo of her palms reverberated around the chamber. She struck her hands again and was astounded by the sound a simple clap made. It sounded as though it were a clap of thunder rather than skin.

The stone around the site had been subject to blasting, and on the floor were deposits of shingle shoved into mounds. Nash could see the large indentations of a digger's tyres in the soil from where the huge buckets shifted the broken stone. Nash could see what she suspected was Moretti's target. The black outline of a soldier, mouth open as if shouting, carrying a rifle. Moretti had said to her how he'd wished he had stood on the right where the wind would have helped him hit his target.

The target on the left, where Boyle had shot, told a different story. There was a small cluster of holes where the heart would've been. Impressive when she considered they were outdoors with all the elements to contend with. Nash moved closer to the wall of rock and let her fingers run over it as she walked. There was dampness to the wall thanks to a recent downpour. As she moved, she noticed part of the shale appeared darker. It was as though the shots Boyle had taken on the paper target against the wooden board had resulted in a spray of blood against the stone. Nash stepped back. Her imagination was working overtime, seeing blood in places where others would see it for what it was – a darker patch of damp within the wall of rock.

Nash left the quarry and walked back to the cottage. It was a twenty-minute jaunt, and she was thankful for the homesteading at the end as she opened the door and stepped inside. As she did, there was a loud crack. The sound made her flinch, and she froze where she stood. Her heart raced as though she was still in mid-run. This was how she remained for a beat. The momentary pause was broken by the low rumble of thunder accompanied by a dark shadow cast over the living room floor where she stood by the only window. The glass pane was hammered upon by a sudden downpour of water as the dark skies rent their angst upon the earth.

Chapter Twenty-Three

Moretti had discharged Matthews from the duty of visiting the wife of Scott Whittaker. His recent marital difficulties and the delicacy of the visit didn't sit well with Moretti. Matthews wasn't upset or unstable, far from it, but he had too much on his mind of a personal nature. If Nash were here, she'd be with him or she'd insist he take another DC along. Moretti wasn't Nash, and that was why they worked so well together.

He hadn't called ahead to Lorraine Whittaker, preferring the element of surprise, or shock and awe as he liked to call it. As he rang the door to her flat, he could hear the sound of a child crying. He checked his watch. It wasn't lunchtime, so he hoped that she wouldn't use that as an excuse. Finally, the door opened.

Lorraine was as poetic in her greeting as she had been the last time.

'Not you again,' she said.

Moretti stood on her welcome mat that framed the outside of the door.

'I'm afraid so, Lorraine. Wondered if we might have a little chat? So much better in person than by phone – wouldn't you agree?' Moretti said as the crying voice became louder.

Lorraine shook her head and walked away, leaving the door open. Moretti took that to be an invitation in and followed her. The place was as it had been the last time. Neat, ordered, and furnished with attention to detail. He walked down the hall and found Lorraine with her child on the floor. A section of which was occupied by a play mat and an assortment of wooden toys. No plastic in Lorraine Whittaker's world unless it was a credit card, Moretti mused, as he sat opposite her.

'I don't have long. We have a playgroup to attend and I don't want to be late,' she said, passing a toy to the child.

Moretti had no intention of outstaying his begrudged welcome. He clasped his hands together as he spoke.

'I need to ask you about the nuisance calls you reported three years ago, shortly after Scott's death,' Moretti said, watching Lorraine's reaction like a hawk tracks a rodent.

'I know when it was. Why are you concerned in an unrelated matter?' she asked, her eyes only watchful of the baby and not looking back at his.

'How do you know the two aren't connected, Lorraine?' he said.

Lorraine sat back in her seat; her head dipped slightly as though she were peering over a pair of reading glasses she wasn't wearing.

'That matter was investigated by the local station and nothing came of it. Probably a case of mistaken identity or some stalker who'd got my number from a bent copper or the press,' she said, looking round as though she'd mislaid an object.

Moretti hadn't seen the object she sought, but he knew the smell of smoke better than anyone and it was a new addition to the house since the last visit. Moretti nodded at where the opened box of cigarettes sat next to a glass ashtray. She placed the cigarette in her mouth and Moretti was there, Zippo in hand, and lit it for her. He sat back down and waited for her to take a few drags before he continued. Lorraine was riled. She was hiding something, and Moretti was determined to establish what that was before he left.

'I'm sorry,' she said. 'I've not been sleeping since you turned up the last time. So much came back to me that I thought had gone... happy times... family times,' she said as she blew smoke away from the baby.

Her eyes came to rest on a photo of her and Scott. A new addition to her cabinet of memoriam, as Moretti had remembered it from the last visit. How death could change what was once a display of memories to a display befitting a mausoleum.

'I'm not going away, Lorraine. Not until we've established who killed Scott and why. I think you're holding onto something... something you really want to talk about but won't. I'll find out either with your help or without it. I can assure you it would be better with it,'

Moretti said, his voice low, even, and calm. It was as though he were talking to the child at her feet rather than the parent charged with his care.

'Well, you're only winding yourself up, officer, as I have nothing to tell you that I haven't already. Now I must be getting the little one ready to leave,' she said, bending to pick him up from the floor.

'Who made those calls?'

'I've no idea.' She gathered the child close and stroked his nose, which he giggled at.

'I think you do know, Lorraine, and I need to speak to that person,' Moretti said.

Moretti could see he'd hit a nerve by the dilation of Lorraine's pupils.

'You need to leave. Now,' she demanded.

Moretti weighed up his options. He could press ahead but that could end up upsetting the child, or he could retreat now and let her stew on it before he returned. He knew that if he came back, then he might have to be prepared to take her to the station rather than a not-so-cosy chat in her front room.

'Lorraine, think about what I've said. I wouldn't be here unless it was necessary. If you choose to leave it, then the next time won't be the same. I have reason to think that whoever was calling may, and I stress *may,* know, or be connected to Scott's killer. Think about that. I'll leave you my number on this card should you change your mind. My phone is always on, Lorraine,' Moretti said. He got up and saw himself out.

He found a cafe and decided to take five before he ventured back to the office. He knew it was a habit of Nash's too. Whenever she sought space, she'd be found at the coffee house across the road from the base along with a host of other addled DIs, all seeking solace and clarity at the bottom of a latte. Moretti ordered a black coffee and found a table nestled in a corner of the minimal eating area. He brought out his phone and began to scroll through the images of Scotland and Northern Ireland as he waited for the coffee to arrive. As he did, he discovered he'd captured a still frame from the quad bike video while he'd been watching it the previous night. It was an obscure capture he put down to being drunk. The frame showed a section of Boyle's truck and the passenger seat that was adorned with the reflective vest.

He stared at it and muttered his thanks to the waitress as she set down his mug. He spread his pinched thumb and index finger on the screen to enlarge the image. There was a nametag inside the collar. Not one that had been sewn in, but written in black onto the washing label attached near the neck. He could make out a B but nothing more due to the fold of the fabric in the still frame. He placed his phone on the table and the image stared back at him. He struggled to see why it seemed relevant. It was a yellow vest in DC Boyle's truck. The truck that was outside the cottage Boyle was in when they'd arrived. He ran his hands through his hair as he willed the caffeine to hit his synapses and spark him to remember why he'd saved the image.

He knew he'd done it for a reason, as he'd need to operate his iPhone beyond a random stab at the screen to capture the still from the video. He'd also managed to save it to his photo roll on the phone, so he must have had a sound reason for doing so. For the life of him, he couldn't think straight. He remembered picking up the bullet the other night and staring at it drunkenly, and he knew where he'd set it down afterwards, but then he'd woken up in the chair and it had become a hazy blur of alcohol and lament.

He watched the people passing outside the cafe window as he concentrated his mind on the image on his phone. He began to realise the link was with the yellow vest and the yellow vest of the rider on the motorbike.

He wanted to call Nash to bounce ideas around with her. He knew he wanted to impress her by having made headway while she was away. He hoped it would make her want him to stay on and not move to another unit or area of policing. He was burnt out, but what human being wouldn't be if every week they had to face death and killing? Killing in the name of power, money, greed, revenge, or pure stupidity and yet it was the likes of he and Nash that were expected to wave a magic wand over it all and come up with the answers to provide resolution to the innocent left behind. It amazed him his mind could still function, and it was no wonder he sought oblivion when he finally arrived home to his boat.

He put his phone away. He'd planted the seeds and his mind was in the process of cultivation. When his brain was ready, when the seeds of suspicion had germinated, he'd know when to harvest the rich bounty he expected. He downed the last of his coffee and left the change on the table along with a tip and returned to the base.

Chapter Twenty-Four

Nash had showered and eaten and was enjoying listening to Radio 4 on an ancient analogue radio. It was the only technology in the place that could get a signal of any sort. The news announced a victory for the NCA in Operation INVIGOR and their drive to combat immigration crime in the form of trafficked humans for the slave trade. A shame they hadn't saved the unidentified male that had ended up here, she thought as she leant on the kitchen table and listened to the rain drum its own paradiddle against the roof and windows. How could anyone live so remotely and not go insane?

She'd loved the run, and it had given her a blast of clean air and her muscles a workout. Too much travel and not enough exercise had taken its toll on her, a woman who considered mental and physical wellbeing as one of life's priorities.

She stretched her neck and grabbed a bag she'd crammed into her carry-on. Within it was the only means of communication she trusted. She left the cottage and walked over to the barn. She drew back the door and found the quad bike Will had said she could use while she was there. The key engaged, and the engine sparked to life with no issues. She gunned the throttle and checking the fuel was good, she left for higher ground away from the farm.

The rain had dissipated to a drizzle and as she rode, she was thankful to not have a crash helmet on, as a visor would have been obstructed her vision. She avoided the main farm track and enjoyed the feeling of power as the engine throbbed and the chunky tyres of the off-road machine ate through the pasture as it negotiated ruts and dips and grass-covered rock. She checked the clock on the bike's small dash and looked back. There was no one to be seen for miles around. Above her, the sun began to hustle for dominance beyond the grey cloud. She killed the engine and remained sat upon the machine.

Reaching into her bag she pulled out a satellite phone. She extended the thick tubular aerial and looked at the screen as the image of a satellite blinked at her. The brick-like instrument waited to link with the space junk orbiting above. Finally, the bars on the screen lit up and the service provider symbol showed. She went to her contacts and selected number six. Six was the only working number on the contacts list. The rest were dead-lines inputted as a distraction for anyone who might pick the phone up should she lose it. She waited for the connection and after six rings she was through.

'You took your time. How's tricks in Narnia?'

Nash smiled at the sound of a familiar voice.

'I'm alive and well. Here's what I've discovered so far,' Nash said to DS Carl Harris.

Harris worked in the undercover unit of the Metropolitan Police and was Nash's cover officer while she was deployed on behalf of the service. She told him what she knew. Harris listened and made notes. He also digitally recorded the conversation.

Policing is a small world despite numbers and distance. The six degrees of separation was strong in the police, and Harris had an allegiance beyond London.

Harris also knew Greg Fielding. He'd assessed the risk to Nash. Harris knew he couldn't leave her alone with only himself as back-up, and that was something he wasn't prepared to risk his career for.

Nash put the phone away in her bag. It felt good to have Harris on her side should anything adverse occur. She hoped it wouldn't come to that and from what she was seeing while back in Northern Ireland she was of a mind nothing would. The seal around the bunker was a good sign. Business closed.

Chapter Twenty-Five

Moretti arrived back at the incident room. As he entered Nash's office, his heart sank. More paperwork had been dumped on the desk. A paper hill that required his signature. As IO, he also needed to oversee each action and ensure it had been completed satisfactorily before it was closed. He flicked on the radio and AC/DC's *Shot in the Dark* played from the radio station Nash enjoyed. He laughed at how the lyrics matched how he felt. He dumped his coat and prepared to tackle the erstwhile forest that occupied his desk and would do so for many hours to come, he thought. He slumped into the office chair.

There was hope. It came in the form of Matthews who'd appeared at the office door looking clean-shaven and full of expectation.

'I need to come in,' he said, entering without waiting to see if Moretti approved.

Moretti showed Matthews his palms.

'Whoa there, soldier, what's with the haste?'

'A breakthrough, Nick, that's what,' he said, his eyes wide open.

Moretti cocked his head. Whenever Matthews announced he'd made a breakthrough, he was proved right.

'I went back over the police report on the nuisance calls received by Lorraine Whittaker and contacted the officer on the case. He was most helpful. He remembered the job as he too felt Lorraine wasn't being forthcoming with the truth and he hadn't the time to waste with an uncooperative victim.'

Moretti let Matthews run as he was on a roll. Moretti knew how mad he got when he was deep in thought and interrupted.

He continued, 'Anyway, I asked the officer if he had any paperwork generated as a result of the investigation. He said he didn't as it was three years old, but he'd been conscious that something should be kept in case the calls continued and a further investigation was required, so he created a General Registry docket which has been sent over to me.'

Matthews passed Moretti the docket. He leant in as Moretti opened it. On top was a statement which Moretti read through; his eyes scanned over the one side of A4. It was brief and to the point. A standard format. Behind it was phone billing for Lorraine Whittaker's phone that showed a list of numbers, dates, and times.

'You've lost me, Owen,' Moretti said.

Matthews was enjoying his game. 'Turn the statement over,' he said.

Moretti turned it over. The reverse of the statement contained all the personal details of the victim or witness. Moretti's eyes became fixed. He looked up at Matthews, whose face was a picture of glee as he saw that Moretti had seen what he had.

'We need to call Nash,' Moretti said. He got up holding the statement and began to pace the room as he waved the page at Matthews. 'This is great work, Owen, great work.'

Matthews's smile was as electric as his mood. 'I know – I know!' he exclaimed as JJ entered the room and framed the doorway.

'What is?' JJ asked with a degree of hesitation in his voice. Good news to management wasn't always good news to the DCs.

Moretti looked at Matthews. 'Go on, Owen, it was your work,' he said with a nod.

Matthews placed his arms behind his head and crossed his legs.

'Lorraine Whittaker was married before she met Scott.'

JJ still looked puzzled. 'So, I've been married and divorced what's the bigun?' he asked, his eyes roaming between the two DSs.

'But your surname wasn't changed from Boyle,' Matthews announced, his face the happiest Moretti had seen in a long time.

Chapter Twenty-Six

Moretti brought the team to silence. The briefing room was packed with all the members of the team that were available. He wanted them to hear this direct and not third hand. It needed to be kept in-house while the NCA and Fielding were sniffing around their work seeking glory.

Moretti felt impassioned. A sense of self-respect had returned. It was a notion he hadn't considered had left him, but as he looked out at the sea of heads, he felt strong and with a purpose. He realised how Nash must feel whenever she stood here and imparted news of significance. News that could break a case wide open and bring them closer to making an arrest. Not an arrest on weak circumstantial suspicion, but an arrest where the chances of the suspect walking out the station on bail were slim to none.

'Thanks for getting back here so quick. I know what a pain in the arse it is especially when you've just been sent to do something and then you're recalled. This is important and provides the context that's been missing from the Whittaker murder. It also justifies DI Nash's need to visit the other scenes in Scotland and Ireland.'

He paused and shuffled some papers on the table in front of him as he considered his next step. Each DC was looking to him for direction now he'd called them back, and it was imperative he provided it. If they left thinking he could have texted the message, he'd lose their faith. It would be like crying wolf and the other times he'd need them back would result in excuses as to why they couldn't leave what they were doing.

'Owen and his Intel cell have done some excellent work that brings a new angle to the Whittaker enquiry. I'll explain it, and Owen will add anything of importance I may miss. As you already know, Lorraine Whittaker hasn't been cooperative.' He had to wait while murmurs of agreement circulated the room.

'I visited her today in relation to the nuisance calls report she'd made. The timing of the report was interesting, as it was two days after Scott's murder. She began getting silent calls on her mobile phone. At the time she said she didn't know who was making the calls, as the person at the other end said nothing. Her billing tells a different tale, as the duration of the calls doesn't support her account. It's common for the victim to terminate the call immediately when they become aware it's their unwanted caller. Not Lorraine. She seemed to think it was appropriate to spend at least three minutes listening to silence. Three minutes may not appear like a long time but we all know how long a minute can seem in the witness box. Despite my best efforts of persuasion, she wasn't forthcoming in telling me any more than we already know,' Moretti said.

The detectives' eyes were upon him. A good sign.

'Owen did some digging and struck gold. Lorraine was married to someone else before marrying Scott. On her statement for the nuisance calls she provided her previous married name, where her maiden name should have been – Boyle.'

Moretti let that sink in and awaited a reaction to test the active minds of some of his team.

'The surname of the DC in Omagh?' Jonesy asked.

'The very same,' Moretti said.

'The issue we have is this…' He took a breath. He knew he was about to impart information he'd been told to keep quiet. However, in DS Nick Moretti's mind he'd not signed an inclusion notice or memorandum of understanding with Nash or Greg Fielding of the NCA. Moretti had a job to do, and that was to find the killer of Scott Whittaker. A man gunned down on a London street for no reason other than he was in the wrong place at the wrong time. It was Moretti's job, while Nash was away, to ensure all new leads were followed up expeditiously despite the wants and needs of outside law enforcement organisations. That was what he intended to do, and he'd deal with the fallout if any came. Prepared to fall on his sword and move unit or worse if it came to it. He took a breath and explained.

'This investigation has spiralled beyond the M25. Some of you, myself included, thought Nash and me going to Scotland and Northern Ireland was a huge jolly. Chasing a bullet. I know that's the rumour as other murder teams on the command have let me know through funny holiday memes and some not so subtle. However, without Nash's tenacity to go where the evidence takes us, we wouldn't have made this link, and it's a vital link. If this turns out to be a different Boyle family, I'll do George's laundry for a month.'

Sagona looked aghast.

'I don't make bets lightly and I expect nothing in return from any of you lot other than your commitment once we make a full breakthrough and link Lorraine with Northern Ireland and DC Boyle. The NCA is working on a Confidential Operation under the umbrella of Operation INVIGOR. You may have read or heard on the news of one recent result. They had a meeting with Nash and me where we were politely told to find another parade to follow. Well, they don't know us, do they? If they did, they'd know that this team will only ever follow the leads that take us closer to the closure of a case and I'm damned if I'm going to ask you to ignore or sit on this information. Owen's team is establishing when and where Lorraine was married and hopefully, we'll see DC Pete Boyle's name linked. Once that happens things will ramp up and I'll be looking to make an early arrest on suspicion of murder. DC Boyle has access to guns and has the ability to travel. What I don't have is motive, but that will come. I'll update you all once I'm ready. In the meantime, keep to your current actions, and thank you.'

Moretti finished and as he did, there was a new buzz about the room. The detectives were happy, and that made him happy.

He hoped he was right, and it wasn't some coincidence and that another Boyle would crop up. He didn't do his own laundry as it was, and he doubted his cleaner would appreciate George's underwear in addition.

Chapter Twenty-Seven

Moretti felt as though he'd found himself on the precipice of a mountain. A mountain where he could see the summit and just needed to take the right path to the top. Which issue bothering him most? He could defy Nash's request to keep things tight and not to rock the boat, or he could cause a stir capable of capsizing it. As he stood in the smoking area outside the block to the incident room, he tampered down the last of the pouch of rum and whisky tobacco and thought through a reasoned approach to his dilemma.

Nash wasn't here. She was God knows where and uncontactable. He recognised her role wasn't easy although she made it appear so with her direct manner. It was all well and good her suggesting he baby sit the investigation while she was away but life on a murder team was never that simple. He couldn't ignore what Matthews had discovered. Lorraine Whittaker was holding something back, and whatever it was could be the key to why her husband was brutally slain while doing his job.

He lit his pipe, inhaled and held the smoke for a beat within his cheeks then blew it out in one sigh. He had no choice. He couldn't expect to have his team work flat out on the research for Lorraine Whittaker's background and establish this link. It was his ship to captain while Nash was away, and steer it he would. There'd be no lifeboats required on this outing.

As his mind turned to boats, it landed on his own barge. His mooring lease was up. Where he held too many memories and not all of them good. He'd had word of a slot opening up in Hackney Wick. An up-and-coming area thanks to the regeneration of the old Olympic park. Many people were taking to boat living along the river Lea. It was a vibrant and bohemian community he saw himself fitting in with just fine. Fuck it. He'd take the slot, he thought. As Moretti took another inhale, Matthews appeared.

'Jackpot,' Matthews announced, waving another sheet of paper in front of Moretti's face like a fan.

'Finding me or what you've found?' he said.

'What my team has found, Nick. One person doesn't make a team, as you well know,' Matthews said, taking in some secondary smoke and Moretti thought by his second inhale he was enjoying the experience as much as him.

'So what is it?' Moretti asked.

'We were right. Lorraine Whittaker's first marriage had been a long one, but she wasn't married to Pete though – she was married to William Boyle, brother to DC Pete Boyle,' Matthews said, as the line of enquiry unfolded like an origami creation before their eyes.

'William, you say?'

'Yes. They married when she was twenty and then it would appear she came to England from Northern Ireland four years ago. How she met Scott I don't know,' Matthews said.

Moretti looked at the bowl of his pipe. He leant against the wall while Matthews used the step as a seat.

'Where does Scott come into it?' Moretti asked.

'He was on a recovery unit that was national in scope from what I can gather. He could go wherever he was sent, why?'

Moretti used his pipe stem as though it were a laser pointer for the briefing screen.

'Check if he ever went to Northern Ireland. In particular, did he come into contact with Lorraine Whittaker through his work? I need to know why she left her home for Scott. What was it about her marriage that was so bad she couldn't stay?' Moretti asked, reinforcing his questions with the pipe's stem.

'Why don't we bring her in and ask her?' Matthews asked.

Moretti placed the pipe back in his mouth. It was a reasonable question, but Moretti's gut was telling him it would amount to nothing. They needed the answers before they asked her direct questions concerning her marriage.

'We need to know that in advance. Forewarned is forearmed, as it were. She's as forthcoming as an MI5 agent. I don't know where to look, Owen, but that's your domain and there must be some way you can try via the backdoor before we go kicking in the main one,' Moretti said, knocking out the dead leaf from the bowl of his pipe.

Matthews nodded in acknowledgement and they both went their separate ways. Moretti to his car and Matthews back to his desk.

As he got into the car, his own phone vibrated in his jacket pocket. He retrieved it and saw the call was coming from PC Kelly McLachlan's mobile. He hesitated before answering. He didn't need any more headaches as a result of outside forces. His own sense of duty overcame him, and he answered.

'Hello,' he said.

The line was clear, and he could hear the rush of traffic in the background. That wasn't the most distinctive sound. That sound came from the chime of a universally familiar bell. Big Ben. He could hear her voice at the other end in between the midday call to arms from the clock tower. Finally, it subsided, and the traffic noise took over.

'Kelly, why are you in London?' he asked, a note of trepidation in his usually calm voice.

'I had to get away, from Scotland – from everything. You said if I was ever in town to call… well I'm here,' she announced.

Moretti removed the microphone section of the phone away from his mouth as he rubbed his eyes. He could hear her voice calling his name.

'I'm still here. I know where you are. Wait for me under the revolving sign of Scotland Yard, it's close to you. If you can't see it, just ask a copper. I'll be there in' – he looked at his watch – 'forty minutes,' he said.

She acknowledged his instructions and Moretti cruised to the tiger trap gates that would lead him off the base. He rolled the car gently in and as the rear gate closed the front opened. He activated the blue light, and the sirens echoed from the surrounding buildings as he motored towards New Scotland Yard and his next meeting with destiny.

* * *

Moretti killed the two-tones and blue light as he turned right off the slip road and on to Embankment. He let the traffic subside and settled in for the short duration before he drew up outside the latest main headquarters for the Metropolitan Police. Moretti had preferred the old building opposite St James's Park tube station but that had been sold off as part of the money saving plans instilled by the current government under their austerity programme.

McLachlan had chosen to sit opposite NSY and look out at the Thames. A better view, Moretti thought, and more sensible than waiting under the iconic revolving sign. Moretti threw his logbook in the vehicle's window and with a nod at the armed security officer and a flip of his warrant card, he crossed the busy lanes of the main thoroughfare to parliament and sat beside McLachlan.

'Hello, stranger,' he said.

McLachlan's eyes were red. Her face looked ashen and gaunt, as though this was her first outing outdoors after a severe bout of flu. Moretti turned side-on to her.

'What brings you here?' he asked calmly, as he took off his jacket and draped it around her shaking shoulders.

'It's all got out of hand, you know?' she said. She shook her bowed head and placed her palms over her eyes.

Moretti placed a hand on her shoulder, and she began to relax. Her sporadic breaths regulated, and she began to recover her composure. Moretti looked about for somewhere to go that might be warmer. NSY was out of the question.

'Come on, I know where we can talk,' he said, helping her to her feet.

He picked up the sports bag that he assumed contained clothing. It was full and weighed enough that he felt his bicep muscle twinge as he lifted it from the pavement. They crossed the road and Moretti opened the rear door to the car and McLachlan got in. Moretti placed her bag on the front passenger seat, and they set off towards the marina and his boat.

He didn't ask anything as he drove. She was tired and still distraught. He'd established she'd taken the first coach she could get from Scotland to London and hadn't slept or eaten since. They arrived at his boat and McLachlan's eyes lit up at the sight of the vessels that occupied the marina. Moretti showed her into the kitchen and living room.

'Dump your stuff and I'll make us a drink and something to eat,' he said.

He prepared a plate of thick cut ham sandwiches and two teas. He didn't want her drinking while she was still in such a state. She ate and as she relaxed, she began to talk. Moretti set his phones on silent. He'd see the screen light up if it were urgent. For now, he hoped the person he was talking to could enlighten him as to what the hell was going on.

'Thanks for getting me. In all honesty, I didn't know what I'd do once I got here. First time in London. I never realised just how spaced out London is,' she said.

'Spaced out in many ways,' he said. 'So why here? Why now?'

McLachlan set her mug down.

'I had to get away. I've not seen or heard anything from the DI or my snitch on the estate since I phoned you. There're rumours getting bandied about that both have been... taken,' she said, biting her bottom lip. A lip that trembled as she said the words. It was as though she was aware that what she was saying sounded ludicrous, and yet she couldn't shake the reality from her mind.

'What makes you think that? Surely someone knows where DI Gordon is? His wife, kids?' Moretti said gently, trying not to intimidate or make her sound to be disingenuous with her statement.

McLachlan looked up. 'Aye you'd think that, wouldn't you? Truth is, we all thought DI Gordon had just taken short-notice leave. Maybe he had problems at home and didn't want the whole station knowing. His wife called and asked where he was... that's what kicked things off... why I'm here,' she offered.

Moretti sensed she was getting close to the reason why and it would be one he didn't want to hear as he would have to instigate the management of it.

'So... why are you here and not at work or home?' he asked.

'Because I think the rumours are true and he's been taken. Management are keeping things quiet, not going public, as they think it'll all blow over like it's some domestic between man and wife and it's too early to smash the glass and press the button. When I called you, after the snitch went missing, me and Gordon went to see a fella, a Vietnamese big shot that DI Gordon says is up to shite but can't prove it. He spoke to this guy outside some work premises, a warehouse in Glasgow. I heard Gordon tell him to wind his neck in and move on or he'd be back with more than just me and he wouldn't like it.'

She paused and lifted her mug. Her hands shook and Moretti knew what was coming next.

'What was he wearing when he spoke to this fella?' he asked.

'What he always wears, a long tan coat and a beanie hat. I swear they're the only outdoor clothes he owns,' she said. Her eyes raised and fell.

Moretti now knew who the other male was in the picture Fielding had shown him and Nash. So, DI Gordon wasn't the obstructive bastard he came across as. He was another detective trying to do his job, keeping his manor clear of filth, and in roamed a rat: McLachlan's source who was now missing, along with Gordon whom Moretti and Nash had both been trying to reach but to no avail. Moretti thought it strange that the force was taking such a casual approach to one of their own having gone missing. Gone were the days when a copper could drift about without checking in – mental health and welfare being a prime concern, and rightly so. Moretti wasn't convinced. Someone must know where he was, along with her snitch, and that person was Fielding of the NCA.

'Do you feel you're next? Because you were with DI Gordon when he confronted this male and now you're here seeking a place of safety?' Moretti said.

McLachlan nodded and looked away from Moretti out of the living room window that provided a vista of the water.

Moretti let his head hang over the rear of his seat. He stared at his ceiling and thought through what he should do. The Met had a witness protection programme but that would be useless in the circumstances as nothing she was fleeing from was reported. It all amounted to supposition, but from what Moretti knew he felt McLachlan had been shrewd in getting away. Better a neutral place than anything associated with her own family. Now he was faced with where she should stay while he sorted this out. He knew what he must do, and that was cover his arse. This had all the makings of an inter-force bomb to which he held the fuse, detonator, and explosives all on his own boat. Problem was he could think of no other options other than her staying with him. He'd at least know where she was. Fuck it, he thought.

'Give me your phones. You can stay here for now. I'll give you a number you can contact me on. I'm afraid you'll have to be uncontactable for the time being while I decide where we go from here,' he said.

McLachlan passed him her phone. Moretti turned it off and removed the SIM card. He walked over to a cabinet. Within it was a small safe, and he placed both card and phone inside and locked it.

'I'm sorry, but I have to consider my own safety as well as yours. It's not that I don't trust you but better safe than sorry,' he said.

She nodded her understanding.

'There's food and drink in the kitchen and you can sleep in the spare room. I'll take your stuff. He grabbed her bag and as he was about to move, he felt arms around his shoulders, and he stopped as McLachlan hugged him.

'Thank you, Nick. I can't tell you how much better I feel now I'm away from there,' she said. She let him go and Moretti continued with his butler role.

He left her on the boat and as he walked back to his car, he wondered if she'd told anyone that she was leaving. He hadn't asked as his mind was awash with so much shit he now had to manage, and he wished Nash was back. He got into his car and set the postcode for the NCA building on his phone. The directions were announced and his time of arrival.

'I'll be way quicker than that,' he announced to himself. The lights in the grill swirled blue and the grit of the road flew up as the rear wheels span and he accelerated out of the marina car park. As he reached the road, he pressed the switch for the sirens and the air filled with the sound of urgency.

Chapter Twenty-Eight

Nash secreted the sat phone in a cutaway in her suitcase. She locked the main lid and put it back on top of the wardrobe where she'd kept it since her arrival.

There was no sign of Will – no sound of a quad bike on the farm and no other engine at all for that matter. It was as though the land had been abandoned since her arrival. She'd been tempted to call Moretti, but she'd resisted. It wasn't required and not on plan. She didn't need to know what was happening at the coalface, her own issues were big enough to contend with.

She sat at the kitchen table and contemplated how to spend her time when the sound of an engine broke her serenity. It wasn't a motorbike or a quad bike. It was meatier in grunt and sounded like a truck. She got up and went to the living room window that backed onto the open land.

It was the same truck that had been outside when she and Moretti had first arrived with Will. DC Boyle must have returned from his excursions, she thought, as the truck drew nearer. As it got close, she glimpsed the driver. It was Will, and he was alone. She backed away from the window as the truck drew up outside the cottage. There was a brief murmur from the engine and then it cut. A single slam of a door told her she was right; Will was alone. There was nothing aggressive in the tone of the door's closure. With it being so windy, it was common for the breeze to catch an open door and close it for you. There was a tap on the door and Nash opened it.

'Now then, Pip. I've brought dinner if you fancy it?' he said, holding what looked to Nash like roadkill.

Nash leant back as Will strode past. The limp neck of the pheasant swung as he strolled past her and into the kitchen.

'Come in,' Nash whispered to herself, closing the door.

Nash paused for a moment before she entered the kitchen. She checked herself in a hall mirror. It wasn't out of vanity or a requirement to impress her imposed guest. This was a ritual she conducted in the privacy of the women's bathroom prior to any interview or during an undercover deployment where possible. She wanted to look herself in the eyes and reassure herself she was in control. She walked into the kitchen just as the cleaver hammered down upon the bird's neck, separating it from the body.

'Jesus! A warning would have been nice,' Nash announced, turning her eyes from the carnage.

Will tossed the severed remnants into a waste bin. He'd been swift in his prep. A wooden chopping board was out that Nash was unaware existed. She'd also never seen the meat cleaver and assumed he'd brought that in the game bag he'd worn strapped across his body.

'Where did you get it?' she asked, hoping he would say a butcher or a nearby country estate used for shooting. Anything other than a B road would appeal more to her. She wasn't a prude, far from it, she'd eaten worse from dodgy stalls and kebab houses in London.

Will smiled and gave a short laugh.

'Don't worry, Pip, it's not come from under the wheels of any truck,' he said, laughing to himself as he continued with the bird's transformation – from a thing of beauty to skin and bone for the oven.

Nash told herself to relax. It was nice to be cooked for. The last occasion had been when she'd been away with Adam Sharpe.

She walked to a cupboard and brought out a bottle of red wine and drew the cork. Will nodded acknowledgement as he raised his glass. 'Slainte,' he said, taking a good slug of the grape.

He was a strange one to fathom. He was calm and relaxed whenever she'd been in his company and had always acted the gent whenever he could. As he cruised the diminutive cottage kitchen, he knew where everything should be, and he'd clearly gone to a great deal of trouble to provide a meal for them as the game bag also held vegetables and other accompaniments to go with the main attraction.

'Have you always been handy in the kitchen?' Nash asked, perching on a stool while she watched Will work.

'I had to become proficient, let's say.' He didn't elaborate and continued to dice some red cabbage.

'You have a knack with a knife,' Nash said.

His hands that had been swift with the blade stopped. It was a brief interlude and then they continued. His eyes concentrating on the task as his knuckles stayed clear of the blade's honed edge.

Nash looked away. Her scar site twinged as the light from outside caught the steel. Her mind returned to her last encounter with a knifeman, but he certainly had no aspirations of becoming a chef. He had intended to carve her up though. She focused her attention on the stove and the pan Will had set to boil. Outside, the rain had stopped and a band of grey mist drifted over the mountains.

'Have you ever married, Pip?'

She snapped back to the present and took another drink before she answered. She wasn't used to being questioned.

'No. I came close, but it wasn't for me,' she said.

'Oh! How close was close?' he asked, as he moved to the pan and dropped some diced potato in to boil.

Nash wondered how much she should let him know. She was happy to share his bounty, but she wouldn't be sharing her bed. If this was Will's attempt at flirting, then she would have to make it clear at some point what she had planned for her evening. An evening she intended to enjoy alone.

'As close as shopping for the ring. He was a soldier in Afghanistan and that was his last tour,' she said. She topped up her mug with wine and added more once she remembered there was another in the pantry.

Will stopped what he was doing and sat across the table from her. He wiped his hands on a tea towel he had tucked into the top of his belt.

'When you say his last tour... I take it you mean he never came back?' he asked, a note of hesitation in his voice as he posed the question.

Nash nodded and Will shook his head as though he'd just been told a prize ewe wasn't pregnant.

'I'm very sorry to hear that. I don't mean to pry. I just couldn't help it. You see, I was married... but there wasn't the commitment I'd been taught came with the sanctity of that union,' he said, withdrawing his lips towards his wine-stained teeth then releasing them.

Nash didn't react. She didn't want to go where he was going, but she knew she had to. She waited, and thankfully Will continued.

'Our ma always taught us that marriage was a one-time thing. Once and once only. Till death us do part.' He let the phrase linger and Nash swallowed.

There had been a shift in his demeanour. She waited for him to continue. He was looking into his mug and swirling the liquid as he mused.

'She left me... left me for a better life. A life away from sheep shit and these rolling planes. She wanted adventure, not a life of solitude and farming,' he said.

Nash shifted in her seat.

'I'm sorry. It can't be easy running everything yourself,' she replied.

Will looked up. His pupils dilated and his eyes flared along with his nose as his lips quivered.

'It's like waking up in hell every bloody day. I reach out and she's not there. I come down to a cold and empty shell that was once a warm and loving home I'd planned to raise a family in. A family to take the Boyle name forward and keep its heritage associated with this land. Now what? I'll tell you – the farm's dead. As dead as that Vietnamese waster who decided to desecrate my soil with his filthy weed. As for my dear brother – the one who made a go of it all beyond the dyke walls – well he's all right, Jack. A healthy pension in a month, so he has, and then he's off to the warmth of Australia to a security consultant job he's wrangled – leaving me here to keep the family name alive until I die,' he said, tipping back his mug and downing the wine before he slammed the container onto the table.

Nash didn't flinch. She'd read Will's body language and remained calm and alert. The fuse had been lit, and she wondered how long there was left of it to burn before the blast came. She had no desire to witness it or get caught up in the back draft.

Chapter Twenty-Nine

'As I've repeated, Acting Detective Inspector, you will go no further than this reception area without an appointment and there's nothing on my ledger to say you're meeting agent Fielding today or any day this week for that matter,' the burly receptionist at the NCA front desk said.

Moretti paced the floor, holding his hair in his hands. He was exasperated with the bullshit he was being subjected to in order to speak with Greg Fielding. The front of house officer was a solid-looking guy in his late fifties. He had greying short back and sides and a beard that was full and well groomed. He looked like ex job who'd taken up the post on retirement.

He'd tried Fielding's phone, but it went to answering machine and no one there was about to give him any information as to whether he was in work, or not, let alone in the UK. Moretti left the building and walked the street.

He found a bench in a park area and contemplated his next move. He was reluctant to drag Lorraine Whittaker in for questioning. Matthews hadn't called him back with any progress on the background research he'd requested. Surely Nash must have had more on Lorraine when the enquiry broke? Maybe she didn't? It was entirely plausible it was treated as a random drive-by shooting and a case of mistaken identity. That was how the investigation was written up. The source unit had had little luck in getting any new leads despite the reward on offer for the recovery of the gun. There'd been some chatter, but the handler had assessed it as rubbish.

Moretti stared across the park. A group of adults were playing a game of football and carrying on without a care in the world. Cafe workers stood at the back of their premises and took smoke breaks. Everyone apart from him seemed to have their lives in order. All under control with no worries in the world. His phone vibrated, and he retrieved it, it was a number he didn't recognise.

'Hello,' he said, waiting for the caller to identify themselves.

'Mr Moretti, this is Greg, I understand you've been looking for me?'

Moretti stood, phone at his ear.

'Where are you? We need to meet and fast,' Moretti demanded.

There was a pause on the other end of the line, and Moretti felt the connection was fading in and out.

'Look, Nick, I can't see you. I'm operationally deployed and—'

Moretti interrupted him mid-sentence.

'Don't give me that "operationally deployed" shit, Greg. I have PC McLachlan at my house crapping herself because she thinks she's about to be kidnapped or worse. My DI has fucked off on leave and I can't make contact with her, and my DCI is a waste of space – so you're it. What's going on? What do you want me to do with McLachlan?' Moretti snapped.

The football game had quietened down and Moretti moved away as he'd raised his voice more than he should have. Greg came back on the line, his manner one of calm and assurance.

'Nick, you've done the right thing by reaching out to me and I appreciate that. We're on the cusp of moving to an arrest phase on the operation we discussed. I can't say too much on an open line. What I can tell you is that PC McLachlan doesn't pose a threat to you. You did the right thing in keeping her safe and calling me. As for DI Nash, I can assure you she'd be supportive of your actions. I need twenty-four hours. By then I'll have the answers to your problem. In the meantime, please leave your phone on, and DS Moretti… do not take any action with Lorraine Whittaker. I cannot stress how important this is. I must go, I'll be in touch,' with that the line went dead.

Moretti looked at the screen of his phone. How did he know about Lorraine Whittaker? Moretti's head was a mess of confusion as to what he should do. He thought about what Fielding had said about Nash being supportive of him and again wondered how he could possibly make that assumption as he'd only met her once.

Moretti had no choice. He'd give Fielding his twenty-four hours and if he'd heard nothing by then he'd have to knock on DCI Carlson's door and that always resulted in untold misery for everyone, as the man hadn't a clue about what they were dealing with from one day to the next. He was so reliant on his DIs to run the show and provide him with all he needed to know to satisfy the ranks above him that it had all become about statistics to him. If the detections were up and the murder rate falling, then he was happy. It was all wrong and as Moretti ambled back towards his car he felt alone, very alone.

* * *

Moretti found Matthews at the office and they sat down together in the canteen. Matthews got the coffees in and joined him at a table tucked away in the corner of the busy and vibrant room.

'Penny for them?' Matthews said, putting the mug down and slopping coffee over the side.

Moretti dumped the mug on a napkin to soak up the spillage.

'Do you ever question why we do this?' Moretti asked.

Matthews shrugged.

'Every bloody day. It's like one step forward twenty back and then we end up with a decent bit of DNA or a confession. I take it you're talking about the Whittaker job?' Matthews asked.

Moretti sighed.

'Murder in general really. I feel like I'm chasing my tail on enquiries and getting nowhere. No sooner have I completed one then another comes along and off we go again in the hope of nipping it in the bud quickly before the next job comes in. Any news your end?' he asked.

'I had a call shortly before you returned. It was from the NCA asking why I was looking at Lorraine Whittaker and her phone data. I never said why, but the agent began talking about remits and crossover of investigations. You know, blue on blue rubbish and how we should cease and desist with our trawling,' Matthews said.

Moretti sat quietly and digested what Matthews had said. So the NCA also had an interest in Lorraine Whittaker. The question was why? They'd expressed no interest when Scott had been shot, as there was nothing in the investigation that showed any liaison. Even if there'd been an operation that was paper only and not on computer, Nash would've known and would've told him. Plus she wouldn't have gone to Glasgow and Northern Ireland so quick without them.

No, this was happening because of Matthews's discovery. It had to be. Once Matthews inputted that on the secure servers, then others in the Met would have access to evaluate that intelligence and they'd be duty bound to flag it up to those who'd be interested. That interest would have been conveyed by the NCA to the Met's own Confidential Unit. The Confi unit was a firewall between outside agencies. It couldn't be a coincidence.

'Any more on the Boyle saga?' Moretti asked.

Matthews leant in.

'Yes – but it may not be what you expected,' he said.

They waited for a gaggle of DCs to pass them, and then Matthews continued.

'Lorraine was born and raised in Nottingham. She went on family holidays to the Sperrin mountains. The family would stay at the cottage. That's where she met Will. They stayed in touch and got married. She was twenty. They were married for ten years and then she left. She came to England and met Scott,' he said.

Moretti nodded.

'Hence the reason Lorraine has no Irish accent. So where and when did Lorraine and Scott get married?' Moretti asked.

'They didn't.'

'Eh?'

'Lorraine started using Whittaker's surname. They were never married and I think this is why she used Boyle on the statement form, it being a legal document, I think she panicked when she said her surname was Whittaker so gave her married name in case anything was ever asked. She could claim confusion at the question or some such bollocks,' Matthews offered.

Moretti thought it through. She was still married to William Boyle. She left him for reasons unknown and came to England where she met Scott and they had a child. Maybe she felt guilt at living in sin or for having left her husband? Maybe she hadn't told Scott she was married at all?

'So do you know any more about her?' Moretti asked.

'Still working on that. It's not easy as Lorraine Whittaker isn't exactly forthcoming as to her personal life and the NCA seems to have an issue with us probing into it.'

'Damn right they do. I had to take a pill from Greg Fielding about the very same. She's off limits for twenty-four hours and without Nash here I'm reluctant to go against it. To be fair, Owen, this investigation has turned into a mare's nest when it should've been a straightforward issue of ballistic reports marrying up, finding the gun and a suspect. I wonder if Nash knew all along where this would take us. You know how she rolls with her undercover lot. Sometimes I can't tell whether she's being genuine or not,' he said.

'Look, I'll keep my enquiries going as to Scott's movements with the recovery firm. I've an appointment with them in an hour. Come along if you like?'

Moretti looked at his watch. It was 6 p.m.

'They're working late, aren't they?' he asked.

'They're like us, twenty-four-hour availability three-hundred and sixty-five days a year,' Matthews said, saluting the air with his chin.

Chapter Thirty

Will moved to the living room, and Nash considered whether this would be a good time to leave. This thought was amplified as Nina Simone's voice glided through the cottage. *I Put a Spell on You* the song of choice. Nash hadn't seen any speakers the last time and as she looked, she noticed two small cubes had been placed on a shelf.

Will returned and leant in the doorway to the kitchen.

'Lorraine introduced me to her voice,' he said, nodding his head to the music. Nash froze.

'Who's Lorraine?' she asked, knowing the reply but not wanting to hear it.

'Lorraine was the love of my life, before that bastard took her,' he said.

He returned to chopping with a ferocity that Nash now knew wasn't dissipating his anger. She felt cornered, but not powerless to react.

'That bastard, Scott Whittaker. He had no right taking my Lorraine,' he said. His head dipped.

Nash kept her focus on Will. His body was now taut with rage.

'What happened, Will?'

Will looked across at her from where he leant. The veins in his forearms pumped and the skin of his knuckles were white.

'That's not important. What's important is what you intend to do next, DI Nash. See, I thought it odd that you returned for a second visit. I can only think you intend on destroying all I've built up and maintained over the years. I can't let you do that.' He licked his top lip and swallowed deeply, his concentration firmly on Nash.

Nash assessed her situation: she had the table between them, and Will had the knife close enough to grab and throw.

'Will, I know what it's like to lose someone you love. I also know that things haven't been easy for you while your brother has been running his own business on the farm's land.'

Will looked away. He remained where he was, the knife a moment's breath from being used on her.

'You know nothing. How can you? A city girl who thinks of the country as a break from her weary lifestyle. Yet here you are, and you can't relax. Your mind wound as tight as the suspension on my tractor. Just like Lorraine's was. She couldn't hack it here either. She was always flighty and desired the trappings of the city. She couldn't take the daily drudge of farm life, the stress of not knowing when your next payment would come or whether you'd have to fold that year or not.' He paused and looked out the window.

It was darker outside. The pot he'd put on had boiled dry. The oven was active, and Nash could smell the bird cooking.

Will continued. 'It was her favourite meal, the one I'm doing for us. It was also the last one we ate together before she left. I didn't know it would be our last supper when she set off in her car. Said she needed to go shopping. She never came back. I got my brother to do some digging. He found out she'd broken down when she left the ferry. That's when she met her shining knight in yellow armour. Scott the brave. Rode up in his mighty recovery truck and the rest is history,' he said. He observed the cleaver examining the rivulets of blood that ran along the blade.

Nash had an idea what was coming and didn't need a seer to tell her.

'Will… step away from the knife, you're frightening me. I know you don't mean to.'

'Pippa, we're going to eat what I've gone to the trouble of cooking, then I'll tell you what you need to know,' he said. He grimaced and his stained teeth withdrew to expose his dark tongue as he held his head back and laughed.

Chapter Thirty-One

Moretti and Matthews spread out the images on Nash's desk. Images from Whittaker's murder as well as images Moretti had taken when he was in Northern Ireland.

The meeting at Scott's firm had gone better than expected. Apparently, Scott met Lorraine by chance after she'd broken down at the ferry point in Cairnryan. Scott was travelling as a foot passenger returning from a visit to Belfast and had seen Lorraine was struggling with her vehicle. The bonnet was up on the car and he'd gone across to help her. The person Moretti and Matthews had spoken to said Lorraine had explained this to the original officers at the time of the murder. They'd wanted background about Scott, and she'd supplied it.

'Why are we viewing these images again?' Matthews questioned.

'We're doing this because there's something about these images that triggered something, but I can't remember why,' Moretti said.

Matthews continued to pick them up and place them down until he reached the one Moretti had captured as a still from his video clip after his bike ride.

'What have you found?' he asked Matthews.

'When did you take this one?' Matthews asked.

'It's a still from a video clip I took while we were on the quad bikes in Northern Ireland. Random, I know,' he said, quietly optimistic that Matthews had noticed something.

'No – it's not random, look what it's of.' Matthews pointed at the image of the yellow jacket and the curled-up tag that displayed the letter B.

'I'm not with you,' Moretti said.

Mathews tapped the print against his hand.

'You travelled from the farm to the cottage by quad bike?'

'Yes.'

'As did Will?'

'Yeah, he was leading us.' Moretti paused from what he was doing and concentrated on Matthews's train of thought.

'So the truck he collected you in he left where?'

'At the farmhouse. He checked the sheep then we all left for the cottage, why?' Moretti questioned.

'You said that DC Boyle was at the cottage when you arrived?'

'That's right. His truck was parked outside. That still is the last frame of the clip,' Moretti said.

Matthews grinned.

'That wasn't Pete Boyle's truck... that was Will or Bill's truck. This is the vest belonging to William or Bill Boyle,' Matthews said.

Moretti pinched the bridge of his nose.

'I don't understand, Owen, it's just a reflective vest. They carry them there because it's so dark that if they break down, they could get run over. Will even put one on me when I was blitzed, and he rolled me down the hill to the cottage after the last night out. He said he'd had to, or he couldn't see me, why?'

Matthews sat on the edge of Nash's desk; his mind churned then his head rose up. A realisation dropped like a winning row of bells on a slot machine.

'Nick, why did we have to wear a reflective vest when we were in uniform?'

Moretti mused before he replied. 'To be seen – to be visible,' he said, still not sure Matthews was on the right track.

'Exactly. So why would our killer wear a reflective vest on a drive-by shooting?' Matthews asked.

Moretti sat back and scratched his neck in thought.

'You tell me, Owen.'

Matthews got off the desk and showed the photo of the CCTV image of the rider and killer in the vest.

'Because that's what we are being asked to see by the killer. It blends in, it looks official, and our eyes go to that and away from the gun about to be fired – it's a perfect ploy to distract any witness. Do you not see, Nick, all the statements describe the shooter wearing a vest but none can describe his facial features, the index of the bike, or the gun they fired. The CCTV from the ports authority in Northern Ireland shows a male being collected from a carpark wearing a yellow vest. Someone rode the bike onto the ferry while the other went on as a foot passenger. A planned action in case the ports had been alerted and were on the lookout for two males on a motorbike, one wearing a reflective vest,' Matthews said.

They both used the lull in conversation to think through Matthews's deduction. It was a stretch to think that Will was a killer just because he owned a yellow vest. Moretti brought out his daybook and scribbled some notes.

'I'll need to talk to someone else before I decide what to do. Someone Nash trusts more than anyone, someone whose opinion she values who isn't in our game,' he said. He got up and went to the desk phone. He lifted the handset and punched in digits and waited. Three rings. A record for this individual.

'Harris,' came back the dulcet tones of the man Moretti wanted.

'Carl, it's Nick Moretti; I could do with a chat. I'd value your input,' Moretti said, listening to breathing the other end.

'The shit really must have hit the fan – my office in an hour? Bring the coffees,' Harris said. The line went dead.

Chapter Thirty-Two

Will looked at the timer on the oven. Nash used the lull to piece together what she knew. She knew that Scott wasn't a random hit but hadn't been able to find a link back to Will. That was until the NCA had contacted her with the information about the Beretta having resurfaced in their Operation INVIGOR. DS Carl Harris had been working alongside the NCA agents. Greg Fielding had wanted an experienced undercover officer to penetrate the group, such was the enormity of the investigation and the many links that spiralled out from the centre thanks to the weapon being used numerous times to kill. Harris had agreed as he fancied a spin with them to see how they operated. When he heard about Nash's investigation, he'd told Fielding she must be included. Harris knew that as soon as Nash became aware of a link to her murder, which she would, she'd be all over it. He was right and Fielding had played his part as had Nash in making it all look so natural in its resurrection.

Nash wanted to find Scott's killer more than anything. She also had a strong desire to get the famous Beretta off the streets and out of the killer's hands. Killer in the singular. She had a hunch which was more than mere supposition, that whoever had the gun was trusted and this was why it had been used on so many streets across the country. The killer was respected enough to be trusted with the gun. A killer who'd evaded forces nationwide and was so notorious that the NCA had got involved thanks to the crossover with their work targeting people traffickers. As she sat across the table, wine untouched, she wondered just how someone like Will had become embroiled in this web of deceit. Will wasn't a drug dealer or a gunslinger, but he was up to his eyes in shit, Nash knew it.

'You're wrong about Lorraine,' Nash said.

Will dropped the cleaver into the deep butler sink.

'Am I? Is that the informed opinion of the city girl who knows fuck all about rural life or marriage?' Will bawled, spittle forming at the creases of his lips. His eyes bulged like a bull on speed.

Nash didn't react. She remained impassive and hoped this wouldn't inflame the situation she found herself in. She chose to continue.

'Scott was a foot passenger on the same ferry your wife was on when he met her. He went to help her as she'd broken down. She asked for his contact details, and he obliged along with the name of the recovery firm where he worked. But you know that. That's why you knew where to go to watch him collect his truck. That's how you followed him from his base until he'd done his last drop off before you gunned him down in cold blood. How do I know? It's called convoy analysis, Will. You weren't sloppy; I'll give you that. You cloned a motorbike and followed Scott while he was out. You managed that for a week, watching him as he went back to his place where Lorraine now lived. You can learn a lot about someone when they offer you a lift because your car's broken down – they had time to talk in the car as they followed the recovery vehicle Scott had arranged. Scott was staying in Newton Stewart with family before he travelled back to London. He'd agreed to take her to a hotel where she could stay until her car was fixed. I think she was taking a breath of fresh air and would've returned, Will. She just needed space. But you started calling, and it all went downhill.'

Will smirked.

'All wrapped up like a gift, DI Nash. So what number was I calling Lorraine off? You've seen I don't carry a phone as it's useless and I'd hardly use my landline, would

I? Not someone who's gone to so much *subterfuge* as you've pointed out,' he said.

Nash sighed. 'Even the best mess up, Will, but that's OK. It's all part of the game we play,' she said. She produced the mobile number Will had left with the eggs in case she needed to get hold of him.

'This is the mobile number you left me in case of emergency. You knew it was useless. I couldn't call you unless I drove miles to get a signal,' Nash said and waited.

Will nodded his head and wagged his index finger in front of his nose.

'You have a memory for numbers, so you do, I'll give you that. Those calls to Lorraine were a long time ago. I was hurting then, knowing how she'd moved on with a mechanic. Ha! I remember having to drive miles just to get a signal on the damn thing, but it was worth it. Worth it to mess with her head like she'd messed with mine. I needed to hear she was suffering the loss in the same way I was suffering at losing her.' Will dropped from the table and Nash shifted in her seat ready to react should he approach.

'So, Pippa, what do we do now? All you have is a mobile number used for nuisance calls, I think it's called. You can't prove I killed Scott Whittaker despite your convoy analysis theory. I could have just fancied following him around for a while on a cloned bike. Big deal. My brother's been a huge help, so he has. A good advisor when he's had a few to drink, so he is. As well as how to clone a vehicle, he told me all about the Glasgow investigation too. Nasty business that... and there's fuck all there to link me other than the motorbike I believe? But I don't have that. You've seen what I keep in the shed and those quad bikes are for fields, not drive-by shootings. All very weak, wouldn't you say?'

He lowered the oven door and wafted away the steam from the bird and brought out the roasting tray. He basted the top again while the fat popped from the hot juices and placed it back in.

'Another twenty minutes should see us done,' he said, grabbing the bottle of wine and swigging a mouthful.

'If you tell me why you killed Scott Whittaker, I'll ask the judge to take into consideration your early help,' Nash said.

The oven door slammed closed.

'I'm not helping you. This is your job, not mine. I have a farm to run. If you're convinced I'm your killer, then where's the smoking gun? Nowhere, that's where, along with the bullets from here and Glasgow. All gone. Face it, Detective Inspector, you're left with nothing but a fine bird to eat and maybe, just maybe, a harassment charge from three years ago based on me saying a few things here. But it will be a case of your word against mine. I've never been in bother with the law. I couldn't be with Pete being in the force. No, I'd say it's all looking pretty poor for you.'

He drank some more. The knife was close to his hand as he drummed his fingers on the sink's surface.

'Face it, Pippa, you've nowhere to run from here. No way of putting a call in to your man across the water. For an Italian he's a shit shot, I tell you. Didn't he do national service?' Will scoffed.

Nash ignored him. In many ways he was right. She was trapped, but not as helpless as he assumed. She wished Moretti were there.

Nash started to rise from her seat.

'Whoa there. Did your mother never tell you it was rude to leave the table without asking?' he said, the bottle still in his hand as he looked at the dregs that were left.

Will's eyes looked beyond the boundary of the window towards the path that led to the bunker.

'I was going to get the other bottle,' she said, but she sat back down on the bench that ran the length of the farmhouse table.

She felt vulnerable. Of that there could be no doubt. She made sure Will wasn't watching as she wiped her sweating palms on her jeans. She wanted to keep him on the back foot.

'When we're done, we'll be taking a walk. It will be good for the digestion, and I need a hand to get in the last of the sheep. Only a few that will need killing. The rest are gone,' Will said.

Nash flashed her eyes at the comment.

'You're kidding,' she announced.

Will finally retrieved the bird and placed the tray on a mat on the table.

'No. I'm not one for jokes. If you want to complete your case, then you'll need to take a walk with me,' he said, his attention back to the cooker.

Nash had her chance. It was there right in front of her as his back was turned. She could upend the table and it would pin him in while she ran out. But then she realised she'd be running into his domain. He knew the land like no other and way better than she. Wherever she ran he could follow by bike or truck. She wouldn't get far and if he was, for a brief moment, feeling genuine remorse and wished to absolve himself then she'd have lost everything.

He was a tough one to read. A closed book, despite his chat. Chat that sounded rehearsed to her. It was as though DC Pete Boyle was in the next room drip-feeding what he should say. Nash caught a glint of yellow in her peripheral vision. The doorway to the hall had been creeping open on newly oiled hinges, and her eyes had caught the side of the reflective vest hanging in the hallway. It had been there all along, she surmised.

The main link staring her in the face. She remembered him wearing it when he'd led them down to the cottage from the house on the bikes and finding it on Moretti when he'd rolled him downhill and left him for dead outside. Nash winced at the memory of the battered and bruised Moretti. He'd reported feeling pain a few days later. Will must have booted him down that hill and enjoyed every minute of messing with the detective charged with solving his nemesis's murder. The final cruel act to place upon him the very vest he wore when he'd gunned Scott down in cold blood. Nash knew she had to see this through to the end whatever it took.

She was acutely aware that there had been a number of other occasions where the gun had been used and she wondered how, or if, Will was connected as there was nothing to suggest he had a motive. Even so, Nash was confident Will knew where the Beretta was and who controlled it.

She rubbed her neck and quietly recited a mantra she used before she would begin training. As she focussed on her breathing, she could feel the air flicker over her top lip as she breathed in and its flow out as she expelled it. All was under control. All was in her control. The pieces were slowly falling into place. She was getting closer to solving Scott's murder, and she was satisfied that Will was involved. Whether he pulled the trigger she'd have to prove beyond reasonable doubt. Was he capable of pulling the trigger because of the pain he felt at the betrayal? She needed to be certain.

Chapter Thirty-Three

Harris called Moretti just before he'd set off and instructed him to attend a different office away from Harris's main one. The building Moretti had been told to attend was occupied by various police units that preferred the anonymity of an older London building than the typical modern police station adorned with a blue sign affixed to the wall. Moretti had made an agreement with Matthews that they'd wait until he returned from seeing Harris. Pointless wasting Matthews's time if Harris could help.

They'd agreed that Matthews could continue working on the links he'd come up with to present to Nash upon her return. Those links would show Lorraine Whittaker, Will, and Pete Boyle knew one another and that must take them closer to Scott's killer. Matthews would also present his theory for the reflective vest. A vest Moretti now wished he could get from Ireland.

DS Harris greeted Moretti at reception. The area wasn't as formal as the NCA's for the very reason that the building didn't attract the same attention and those that arrived there, on the whole, had an invitation. Harris handed him a lanyard with paper ID attached in a plastic holder. It contained a number only.

'Stick this on. You'll only get challenged every few steps without it,' Harris said.

They walked across a garden of raised beds towards doors on the opposite side of the courtyard. They entered and went down a flight of stairs towards voices. The canteen was busy with a diverse mix of plain-clothes detectives. Some wore suits, others were dressed as though they could do with a bath. There was the usual raise of eyes towards the stairs as the feet appeared and once those eyes had seen Harris they looked away, satisfied that Moretti was there by design and not fault. They found a set of chairs towards the rear of the canteen and sat down. Moretti had done as Carl asked and brought coffees from outside. Far better than what was served from the machines there.

'So, what's bothering you?' Harris asked, his hand gripping the cardboard cup as he took a sip.

Moretti looked about before he spoke.

'Don't be concerned about who's here, Nick. Everyone knows the score and you can talk freely,' Harris reassured him.

Moretti sat back in his seat and the lines that had formed on his forehead disappeared.

'I'm concerned about Pip. She took off like her arse was on fire and just left me to manage a job that... well, to be frank, has grief written all over it. Problem is, I've come up with more links between this shooting in London we're investigating and another one in Northern Ireland. At least I think I have, and I need to pursue it, but she was adamant I sit tight until she got back. Trouble is, I don't know when that will be,' Moretti said.

Harris nodded, his eyes firmly set on Moretti. Once he was sure Moretti had finished talking, he sat forward and so did Moretti.

'Look, you've nothing to be concerned about with Pip. She's fine,' Harris said.

Moretti looked at Harris and attempted to interpret what he was intimating.

'So... you know where she is?'

Harris wiped his mouth and looked over his shoulder at a couple of senior management in huddled conversation.

'Yes, but I can't say,' Harris said.

'Another of her covert jobs without a by or leave or I'll see you soon. Typical. Why would she leave me, her number two, in the shit while she goes off to play with your lot?' Moretti noticed he'd raised his voice and Harris shot him down with a look.

'Watch your mouth, Nick. I know it's said with the right amount of feeling vis-à-vis respect for Nash but it's the wrong arena here to voice it.'

Harris's phone buzzed and he quickly snapped it up off the table. He grunted a couple of times and then killed the call.

'Fuck it. Come with me and you'd better grab us a sandwich before we go,' Harris said.

Moretti got up shaking his head in confusion and went to purchase whatever was left.

They'd surfaced from the canteen and crossed back to the reception building. Harris took them to the first floor, and told Moretti to wait in a side room while he made a call on an internal line. Harris returned with a small blue crate.

'Place every phone, car key or any other electronic device in here and follow me,' Harris said.

Moretti did as directed. Harris placed the small crate in a locker and lead the way towards another door. He swiped a plastic card across a keypad, punched in the pass code and turned to Moretti.

'We all have Nash and her investigation at the forefront of our minds, Nick. I've got you access in here as you may have something worthwhile to say once we're beyond these doors,' Harris said, and they both entered the room beyond the security keypad.

Moretti's jaw dropped at the bank of monitors on display inside the Secure Covert Operations Facility. The soundproof room had done its job well. He'd heard nothing until the door was opened and a sea of voices entered his brain. Some people were tapping away on keyboards while others equipped with mics monitored a bank of screens. Moretti stopped by a desk where a radio operator was deep in concentration. On the bank of screens in front of Moretti was the face of Nash. Moretti leant on the operator's desk and stared at the screen. The multiple screens became one and Nash was clearly visible sat at a kitchen table in a room Moretti recognised.

'Why in the hell is she there? Alone?' Moretti said.

Harris came alongside him and offered a spare seat for him to sit and observe.

'The operation's been running for months now. I was out there at the inception posing as a middleman for the weed and amphetamine Quan Thao had been distributing. He's a nasty piece of work, Nick. He's been arranging for far too many Vietnamese nationals to be delivered to his empire. They have been abused beyond comprehension. His empire is way beyond what you witnessed in the bunker. That was his smallest grow house and a distraction from his main line of business. Sexual exploitation on a nationwide scale along with the grow houses and amphetamine labs. Even for a hardened bastard like me, it is way beyond anything I'd ever had the misfortune to witness,' Harris said.

Conversation was light as they observed the screen.

Moretti shook his head. 'How on earth did a cold case that amounted to a ballistic link turn into this?'

'When the bullet came back from Scotland, I knew we had an issue. The moment it was linked to one of Nash's cold cases I knew there'd be no stopping her pursuing the evidence. That's one of the reasons she's my best undercover and I don't say that lightly. That's why you *both* went out to Glasgow and then to Northern Ireland. She wouldn't leave her best DS out of the loop entirely. That was her only condition to get involved in the bigger operation. That's why she was pissed at you for getting pissed.' Harris smirked, and Moretti raised his eyes.

The pennies were dropping. It had all seemed too good to be true. Two trips away on the back of a linked shooting with no suspect or gun. Then the disappearance of the victims and the evidence. Moretti was starting to see that the enquiry was larger than he could have imagined.

'So what have you established?' Harris asked.

'Lorraine Whittaker was married to Will Boyle. Also, the yellow vest that I'd inadvertently captured in a stupid video could be relevant. The shooter for Scott and the Glasgow hit was wearing one. Owen Matthews thinks it was to distract any witness's eye from the gun to the vest. Plus, they'd blend in. A jacket for safety. Who'd have thought it could be used as distraction? It was like Scott's killer was hiding in plain sight. Like he wanted to be seen.'

Moretti paused and let his brain turn over all that was coming to the surface.

'Good call. I've seen Matthews's work. I had access to his computer, only for the purposes of oversight, nothing more. This operation you're witness to is off the books, Nick. It's a paper-based operation due to the corruption involved. The sheer scale of Thao's operation would not be possible without those inside our organisations being on the take. Not that Owen Matthews is, he's just doing his job, and very well indeed. DC Boyle is another matter, as is his brother. They are up to their eyes in debt. Both trying to keep the farm and the family name attached to the land. DC Boyle uses the cottage to conduct criminal business and we have sight and sound as you're seeing. It's a royal mess,' Harris said, as they listened to the feed from the cottage.

The room was calmer now and the immediate threat to Nash seemed to have subsided in Pressure Cooker Cottage, as it had been labelled by the Ops team. Moretti could see why.

'So what about the Berretta and the bullets?' Moretti asked.

Harris rubbed his nose before he spoke. 'That's a huge issue. We don't know. What we do know is that DC Pete Boyle is the controller for the weapon and ammo. He has kept it clear of the cottage and the farmhouse. He doesn't keep it at his own property either. His property is pretty grand for a DC. New build and stately. We'll be having that away once this comes to a head,' Harris offered.

'What about the cloned motorbike? It wasn't at the farm…' Moretti's voice trailed off. Harris latched onto the vacant look on Moretti's face.

'Go on, Nick, say what's on your mind,' Harris said.

Greg Fielding entered the secure room and approached them. Harris raised his finger to his lips and Greg nodded.

'I think the motorbike is located at the police station where Boyle works… there's a covered garage area and a bike is under a protective cover. I thought it was odd at the time. Why would you cover a bike that was already protected from the elements,' Moretti said.

'Good work,' Harris said.

Fielding tapped an operator on the shoulder and had a brief conversation as he leant in. The operator picked up a landline and briefed what Moretti surmised was a tactical team on standby. They'd secure the bike if it moved from the station yard at all costs. Moretti was handed a folder by Fielding who sat and joined them. In it was a series of images of blocks of compressed cannabis. Easier to transport.

'Remember O'Connell, our legitimate motorbike owner? Well, look at the logo on the blocks and then turn the page,' Fielding said.

Moretti did as he was asked. On the main page there was an image of what Moretti considered was a bug of some sort in green and black. Then, on the next page, he could see that the bag they'd seized from O'Connell was embossed with the same image.

'This is how far Thao's empire reaches. That sample you found with O'Connell will be linked to the seizure we've just made from a ferry in the Irish Sea. The street value is estimated to be in the millions. The one O'Connell had a purchase from was smaller. A sample from a batch on a test run. Thao decided to switch things up using a different vehicle and method of travel. A sheep trailer that was empty but adapted to carry the drugs compressed into a false wall in the steel frame and underneath the chassis. Not the type of agricultural pursuit we're used to,' Fielding said.

'Quiet please.' The voice of the room's controller was stentorian and firm. Everyone stopped talking, and all eyes were directed at the screen and an image of Will as he brandished the meat cleaver and walked towards Nash.

Chapter Thirty-Four

'Put the knife away, Will. We can talk this through and come to an agreement. Like you said it's just me and you and that's it. You're right, I am just a city girl out of her depth in the country. But it's only me and you, so whatever you tell me I'd have a tough job convincing a jury.' Nash let that settle for a moment.

'I'm not here to make your little holiday a nice one, Pippa. I need the money, but I don't need repeat business from anyone else from London's Metropolitan Police. No – what I need is Lorraine back. And you can't help me with that... not now she has a kid an' all. Too much time has passed to re-kindle what we had and I'm tiring of the games,' he said, holding the cleaver as though he were readying himself to lunge across the table and take off her head.

Nash believed he was capable of such an act. She'd seen a new side to the calm and placid Will Boyle. Will was the archetypal boy-next-door who would go out of his way to help an old lady across the road before he hacked her to death if she said the wrong thing.

Nash was of the opinion she'd run out of options. There was nothing she was saying that would convince him to say where the gun was. She calmed herself for the next move. A move she wished she'd never have to take, as the stakes were high. She'd come to like Will, in a strange way. He was a grafter and from all appearances was doing his best to keep the farm going. Will had murdered Scott, she was as certain as she could be of that now, but she didn't have the evidence to place him at the scene. She also didn't have the gun or the bullets to match. What had seemed a possibility in terms of getting a confession had diminished and as she said her mantra to herself, she knew she had to bring it to an end before Will did.

'Will, I'm sorry but you've crossed the Rubicon and I cannot help you back.' Nash leant down and held her breath.

Chapter Thirty-Five

'Alpha one, code word Rubicon – over to you.'

'Alpha one, code word Rubicon, acknowledged,' came the reply from the NCA sniper who'd been living outdoors and watching the cottage from the ridge. He had a clear and unobstructed view of the kitchen window and his sight was placed on William Boyle who raised the cleaver and stepped towards Nash.

The windowpane shattered, and Nash screamed in shock as Will dropped to the floor in a shower of glass. The shot was clean. Nash opened her eyes to see the shattered skull of Will Boyle against the flagstone floor. She looked away, then got up and went to his side and checked his pulse. Instinct had taken over. Preservation of life despite the ultimate use of force. Nash was angry. The shot was meant to incapacitate, not eliminate. If he had the Beretta that was different but not a knife. She might have got away or used the table as defence.

She felt a hand on her shoulder; she turned quickly to discover what looked like soldiers in the cottage, except they weren't soldiers – they were members of the NCA who'd been living rough while she'd been planted as bait back at the cottage. Bait to lure Will into telling her about the operation his brother was running to provide concrete proof of his criminal activities and find the gun used in the murders. All of that opportunity was now spent as she watched agents secure the cottage and turn off the oven. One of the men pulled off some meat from the cooling pheasant and ate it.

'Sorry but I'm starving, and it smells so good.'

Nash got up and walked out into the fresh air. She looked up the track to where the bunker was and there were flashes of sparks as another team went to work on opening the hatch to the bunker.

After a short duration she heard shouts for ropes and a harness. She waited and slumped down against the wall of the cottage while others swarmed over the once tranquil idyll. Where they'd appeared from, she had no idea, but her mind was so messed up from the experience she felt faint and confused. They all looked like they'd been living rough, and she guessed that they must have been doing so and drew in closer once the Ops room authorised the take down. She'd told them in the planning phase she'd lean down and touch her ear if she'd given the code and the sound was out. If visual and sound were down, she'd have been dead. The NCA had assured her that they had drones and a satellite feed the same as the one linked to her phone. Communication would be effective, and she'd trusted that to be true. Trusted it because more than anything she wanted Scott's killer to stand trial and now that was gone.

Her eyes rose to see the sight of a male being escorted down the path towards the cottage. A male she recognised as DI Gordon. There was also a body being lifted clear of the hatch. That person wasn't as fortunate. The officers laid the male gently onto a stretcher, a dark plastic body bag upon it. From where Nash was, she could see the clothing belonged to the male who'd been stood outside the row of shops in Glasgow. They'd been sick enough to leave Gordon to die with the body of his snitch next to him rather than kill them both. She got up as DI Gordon approached and he looked up wearily at her. He gave her a weak smile and Nash walked forward and hugged him. As they connected, one DI to another, they let their emotions show. They stepped back, and both wiped tears from their eyes.

'Are you all right?' Nash said.

Gordon regained his composure.

'I'll nay recover quickly from that experience or use a tunnel again,' he said. His hand shook as he spoke. The NCA agents supported him as they walked him away to a tented area that had been hastily set up.

Nash realised there was an NCA man stood alongside her. In his hand was a leg of the pheasant.

'How are you?' he asked.

Nash looked away.

'I had to take him out. I felt you were in immediate danger. I know what was agreed but I have a job to do, like you – protect life.'

He left her with those words to find some water from the tent. Nash followed him. She needed to find another sat phone she knew would be in there.

Back in the operations room in London there was a solemn atmosphere. It wasn't how they'd hoped it would all end, but it wasn't all over as the screens that once displayed the cottage were now focussed on the CCTV cameras at Belfast airport fixed on one male: DC Pete Boyle. Boyle wasn't alone as trailing behind him walked Flanagan, his boss. They'd been left to get past the boarding gates and to board the flight to London where they were to board a connecting flight to Sydney via Bangkok. So much for family and farm being such a concern. The controller asked for the monitors to be split and they were. Thao was now on another screen being led from his warehouse in London by plain-clothes armed officers. The same search was being conducted in Glasgow. Shipping containers were being opened where it was hoped the latest human cargo would be discovered and saved.

Across the UK a series of coordinated raids were being executed: warehouses, residential houses, and various properties were being seized and searched. Hundreds of officers deployed to their tasks. One item that was missing was the Berretta and the bullets. Nash waited as the connection to the control room was made. She was placed through to Fielding who congratulated her on her efforts and then handed the phone to Moretti.

'Pip?'

'What a surprise to hear your voice,' she said, with a smirk, relaxing at the sound of his familiar gravelled voice.

'Couldn't miss a good party, Pip, you know me. When are you back?'

Nash looked around her. It wasn't her scene, and she could leave whenever she wanted.

'I'll fly back this evening. I'm sick of the countryside and need a decent curry... if you're up for it?' she said.

'I'll pick you up if you can fly into City Airport. Stay at the boat, Pip, as my houseguest can go home now,' he said.

'The stripper?' Nash enquired.

'No, Pip, it's a long story best shared over a curry and beers,' he replied.

Chapter Thirty-Six

Moretti made swift work of dispatching PC McLachlan back to Glasgow. He dropped her off at the same airport Nash was coming into. Crisis averted, she could return home. He'd let DI Gordon explain to her about her source. Some things were beyond his pay grade and he'd had enough of playing DI.

He'd collected Nash and they'd agreed a takeout would be the best bet and Moretti arranged everything. Nash dumped her stuff in the room McLachlan had vacated. She looked around Moretti's domain and sat down on the bed. She lay her head back against the fresh sheets and covered her eyes with her hands. Her shoulders juddered.

Moretti had followed her into the room to make sure she had everything she needed and was carrying a small box, bow attached, upon plain wrapping paper. He gave a light knock. Nash didn't move. She was too exhausted and knew there was no one else it could be but DS Nick Moretti, her maverick, tempestuous partner in the fight against crime. She'd grown attached to him over the time they'd spent dealing with the worst of what society had become. He sat at the edge of the bed and waited until Nash sat up on her elbows, her eyes red and glazed with tears, fatigue, and angst.

'Sorry. You shouldn't have seen that. I was going to freshen up and come out and help you dish up,' she offered.

Moretti gave her a smile.

'Don't be silly,' he said, tapping the box.

Nash saw it and rose to a full-seated position.

'What lucky lady is that for…?' she asked, her wry smile returning to her defined cheekbones.

Moretti got up as though he was back in the office and paced the room.

'I know how much I've been a… distraction, let's say, through my ways of drink and song,' he mused.

Nash lay back on the pillows and propped her head in her hands as she waited for Moretti's sermon to end.

'I am who I am, Pip, and I can't change that, and won't, not for the sake of this bloody job or you. But I want you to know that I am, and always will be, an advocate of yours and will always have your back,' he said.

He sat back on the bed. Nash felt as though Moretti was building up to telling her he was moving on. She waited, their shoulders touched and neither of them moved.

'Go on,' she said.

'Having had the opportunity to sit where you do, I hated every minute of it. I saw how much you keep from my door, and it was eye opening. I'm a guy who needs to be in among it and I won't be seeking promotion. I'm happy to continue working with you if that's what you wish?'

Before Nash could say anything, he raised his hand.

'I know how much getting the killer for Scott Whittaker's murder meant to you. I've never known another detective go to the lengths you do and place yourself at risk for this job or for any victim and their families. I heard that DC Boyle is pinning everything on Will. How he's adamant Will was a violent man who pushed his brother to commit crime in order to protect the family farm. How poor DC Boyle was an innocent pawn in a cannabis game that got out of hand. I know it's all bollocks but with Will dead he could mount a good case despite what the NCA have on him. I also know the Berretta and the ammo are gone for good now. Boyle told the NCA he'd taken a three-year career break to get away from Will and his obsession with Scott. He put the ownership of the gun on Will and denied any knowledge of it. Even saying Will had been the one to execute the Vietnamese guy in the bunker and claimed Will hadn't seen the body when he had. We'll never know, but what's in the box will help in some way to counter all that.'

Moretti handed Nash the box and she looked at Moretti and down at the gift-wrapped present before her. As she undid the bow Moretti said, 'I heard Will had mentioned how he thought you'd had the case all gift-wrapped... well hopefully he'll be turning in his grave.'

Nash opened the lid and produced a small exhibits bag. In it was the crushed bullet Moretti had taken from the quarry wall where Boyle had been shooting. Alongside it was a memory card. Moretti took the memory card and left the room. He returned with the laptop to an astonished Nash.

'Where did you get this bullet?' she asked.

Moretti told her and inserted the card and pressed play. They both watched a video clip of DC Pete Boyle as he shot using a pistol. He was stood in the prone position and looked ever the good shot he was. Moretti had turned the phone's camera to show himself and Boyle as they walked down to the target where a cluster of holes appeared around the heart. Not a single shot had missed. Nash stopped the recording.

'And this helps *us* how?' she asked.

Moretti smiled.

'I had the lab enhance the last frame. The gun he was firing… was a Beretta. The slug you're holding is from that gun and matches the same batch as that used on Scott Whittaker, the victim in Glasgow, and the Vietnamese male in the bunker. They also believe the same gun that fired this was used in all the other crimes by examination of the bullet in your possession. The bullet – I dug out of the quarry wall. A keepsake of a great time away. Will Boyle would have had an alibi for all the other killings. Pete Boyle chose market day to murder rivals in Thao's empire, knowing Will would be none the wiser. I believe DC Boyle killed Scott Whittaker. Will was the rider to the job. Boyle must have told Will if he ever spoke about the cannabis farm in the bunker, he'd tell the authorities it was Will that killed Scott.'

Moretti looked at her. He felt good to have that off his chest. He hadn't even told her that the NCA had matched the yellow vest from the cottage to the one worn at the Glasgow shoot site. Microscopic flecks of blood were on the front, invisible to the naked eye, and hadn't been lost when Will had rolled Moretti down the hill as they were well and truly dried on, below the surface of the weave.

Nash put the bag on the bed and turned to Moretti. She took his face in her hands and kissed him on his forehead.

'Bloody good work, detective sergeant, now let's eat,' she announced.

They got up off the bed. Both of them felt as though they'd done all that could be done for Scott Whittaker.

Pete Boyle was in custody. The location of the Beretta was still unknown. They knew he'd give up the location sooner or later. Then they'd hit him with what Moretti and the lab had detected. His footage showed Boyle in possession of a weapon he denied knowledge of and yet despite his best attempts to rid himself of the last of the ammo after the two from London had got involved, it had come back to bite him.

They'd get their man even if they had to wait for the dust to settle now the gunshots had subsided.

DC Pete Boyle had more than a missing gun to account for.

Thao was in talks with Fielding after being shown evidence of two shallow graves that contained the bodies of the victims. Both had been removed by Thao's men following contact from DC Boyle. Fielding was in possession of recorded conversations, and surveillance imagery, as a result of the NCA's sensitive operational enquires. Conversations between Boyle and Thao. Photos of both men together, one showing Thao present in a Volvo XC90 when Boyle is seen to hand over police exhibit bags to his driver.

The sheep trailer packed with drugs that was seized on the ferry belonged to Will Boyle. DC Boyle had arranged for Thao's driver to convey the trailer attached to the Volvo for that run. DC Boyle had become too confident the gun was untraceable, and that Thao's empire was untouchable, but as any decent detective knows, when the circumstances are stacked against you it's time to buckle up and enjoy the ride. At some point it all has to come to an end. For DC Pete Boyle the end was but a breath away.

The End

If you enjoyed this book, please let others know by leaving
a quick review on Amazon. Also, if you spot anything
untoward in the paperback, get in touch. We strive for the
best quality and appreciate reader feedback.

editor@thebookfolks.com

ALSO IN THIS SERIES

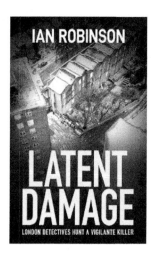

LATENT DAMAGE (book 1)

When a respected member of the community is murdered, it is not the kind of knife crime London detectives DI Nash and DS Moretti are used to dealing with. Someone has an agenda and it is rotten to the core. But catching this killer will take all of their police skills and more.

COVER BLOWN (book 2)

A London advertising executive is found dead in her
bath. Soon another woman is killed in similar
circumstances. DI Nash and DS Moretti are hunting a
killer, but finding a link between the victims is the
only lead. What is it about their social media accounts
that makes them a target?

OTHER TITLES OF INTEREST

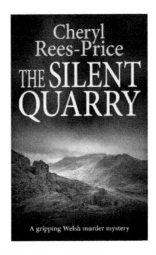

THE SILENT QUARRY by Cheryl Rees-Price

Following a fall and a bang to the head, a woman's memories come flooding back about an incident that occurred twenty years ago in which her friend was murdered. As she pieces together the events and tells the police, she begins to fear repercussions. DI Winter Meadows must work out the identity of the killer before they strike again.

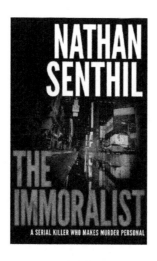

THE IMMORALIST by Nathan Senthil

Self-styled Mr. Bunny wants to be the most notorious
killer in US history. With four high profile figures
slowly hanging to their deaths, he's off to a good
start. NYPD homicide detective Gabriel Chase much
catch him, no matter at what cost. But who will have
the last laugh?

Printed in Great Britain
by Amazon

83789306R00103